# Son Of Malonie

Think more than you speak,
Act more than you say,
Do more than you don't


A person is not built by 'what they are meant to be', but by who they have around them.

*'Nobody is above this family'*

The shiny, doleful ceiling painting of Sage Markandeya, the god of immortality, hung omnipotently over the historic sight of the infamous mobster, Serbeano Malonie, on his death bed.

Surrounded by his brother, Randol, and his son, Michael next to his cousin, Ralph witnessed as his wife, Martha, gave her final kiss before Serbeano softly ordered her out of the room, he never planned business in the presence of a woman as he always argued that women should be loved and not bored in the blood infested business of gangster warfare.

"Randol my brother come here", Serbeano coughed his brother over to his left ear where Randol leant down to listen to his brother's dying request. "You know what you have to do?", whispered Serbeano. "Of course I will make sure it is done". "Good, its time he came home to end this vendetta that has brought us all such pain". "I will make sure he is ready. Thank you for everything you have done Serb, we had a good run me and you, pops would be proud", a tear aimlessly rolled down from Randol's eye. "And Mom. Your moment has come *coughs* to end this war", Serbeano chaotically coughed then died staring up at the immortal image of Markandeya. "From rags to riches", Randol whispered at the sight of his deceased brother.

From that moment, the entirety of New York city knew that date of March 14th was the day a god died.

Every newspaper within the city covered this event, the news coverage covered the story for a whole week, the whole city was in shock and wonder as the man of Serbeano Malonie had died, but the myth still lived. In the midst of the mourning city, crime increased severely as people began to take advantage and claim the superficial title of 'king of the city'.

Serbeano was the man of the city. Alongside his brothers, Randol, and Arty, and his childhood friend, Razor Rully, he ran New York. Although he was born in the USA, his ancestors were Irish, making him Irish-American, fleeing Ireland in 1849 after suffering badly from the potato famine.

Serbeano, Randol, and Arty worked their way up in the city befriending powerful men and gaining their trust, because trust is everything. Their father, Eamon (named after Ireland's first Taoiseach which meant prime minister), was born into the family and lead it as the crime family it was today. Eamon worked hard for the family Serbeano ran, he made many an enemy which left Serbeano struggling to rebuild their trust when he became Don in 1958.

Serbeano was the eldest brother, hence why he was made Don after his father's passing. Randol was the middle child, and Arty was the youngest. The two other brothers always referred to Serbeano as the 'thinker' of the three. He could always talk his way out of an ass-kicking, which payed dividends later in life when it came to negotiating with criminals. Randol was the fiery animal, who became calm and mellow later in life (there's only so much heat the heart can take), and Arty was the muscle, he had no fear in taking another man's life. They soon built their family and legacy.

Serbeano put the Irish-American mafia on the scene, up until that point in New York the Italians ran the city. But when Serbeano made his Irish family famous with the murder of the mayor of New York, Ace Shelby in 1960, he secured the Irish-American reputation as the 'top dogs' of the city. The Italians hated the fact that 'foreigners' were taking over their land and so ensued a three decade long war other families labelled as 'The Irish-Italian Blood Grudge'.

The Malonie family grew and became New York's most respected family. Along with this title came enemies though, siding with police and having them on their pay roll they pissed on the parade of the Italian – American mafia families in New York, making the war even more heated, more specifically the Santana family. Things were made even worse when Randol Malonie aided the police with the arrest of Carlos Santana in 1971. The war still continued to this day in 1982. Enzo Santana avenged this by murdering Arty Malonie. At this point Serbeano knew that this war would only end in pure annihilation of ultimate devastation serving as the conclusion.

The Santana's weren't the only problem our Irish-American mafia family faced. In 1975 Serbeano cut his lifelong friend, Razor Rully, from the family business. He was pressured by the five families to cut Razor loose after Razor had become messy in his actions. He was drinking more and more as well as killing clients on orders 'not to kill'. However, it was the accusation of rape that topped it for Serbeano and the five families. They would do business with ex-convicts, murderers, thieves and fiends but not rapists. A man who doesn't respect women will never be a real man.

Rully brought something different to the world of cold-hearted killing and stealing money, he used to dress like he was the main star of a western film. Donning a white cowboy hat, old boots and always chewing on a toothpick. This came from his fascination of the western classics and made him stand out a mile from the rest. Serbeano never liked the way Rully dressed, he felt it was bringing unnecessary attention to the family and ridiculed them a little. On several occasions Serbeano tried to make Rully change his appearance. This always ended in a heated argument so he gave up after a while.

The main body of the Malonie family consisted of Serbeano and his wife, Martha, their children Salvatore, Michael and Alexa, Randol and his wife Lindsey with their two boys Ralph and Moxie, Arty's sons Sull and Henry, Serb's cousin Johnny and his wife Kath. They also have extended members who are friends of the family which serve as 'helping hands'. To Serbeano, family was everything no situation was bigger than family.

This tale of legacy and family begins with one man. Salvatore Malonie. The son of Malonie...

Serbeano's first born and apparent heir to the Malonie kingdom, Serbeano had sent Salvatore away when he was twenty-eight. He had sent him to London England, this was a result of a vendetta. Serbeano had ordered a hit on Razor Rully, as he was refusing to leave. Razor took them to war burning down their business factories and wanting vigorous vengeance. The hitman hired got the wrong guy and killed Razor's first born, Sully, so Razor made it his mission to kill Salvatore in return. Serbeano didn't want to burry his son so he sent him away and hid him in England. Razor went cold as he continued his never-ending search for Salvatore. This happened five years ago, Sal was informed by his father he could never return unless Razor died.

21st March 1982. The following week came the funeral. Citizens fled the streets, complete randomers who Serbeano had never even met paid their respects. Randol held Martha as the coffin descended into the ground. Sull stood opposite watching the crowd for anyone who wasn't meant to be there. Randol had prepared a speech, he pulls out a small piece of paper from his blazer pocket. It reads; "Serb was a calm man, who helped and had an affect on us all here today in some way or another. He led this family to greatness, always aiding us in our problems and negotiating his way through anything and everything that came his way. His sense of humour was annoying to say the least, pulling pranks on us when we least expect. But when it came to business nobody was better. I feel as though I lost my right arm when he passed. One thing is for sure this family will never be the same again", a tear drops from his eye.

An era had been laid to rest. The streets would be changed forever. There was no Don like Serbeano, he brought something different to the table, he brought a statement of class in his traditional beliefs of family before anything. Loyalty meant the world to the man.

Leaving the church, the citizens began clapping, showing their respect to the 'king of the city'. Five news reporters rushed in and wanted to get words from Randol. The bulky boys, Henry and Sull kept pushing them back but one blonde woman broke through and got to Randol. She went to pull her microphone but instead pulled a revolver, Michael noticed this and pulled his uncle back before hurdling his body at the woman and beating her relentlessly to the point that Ralph had to drag him off. Michael spits on her blooded head. The crowd of citizens gasp in shock and back away. They all play witness to the heinous attack.

Back in the house Randol has called Michael into an empty room in the mansion. "What you did there today was unprofessional. We had citizens watching us", Randol, extremely frustrated with how Michael handled the situation educates. "Are you crazy? I saved your life!", the ever-short tempered Michael rages back, wanting to initiate a verbal war with his uncle. "One hit would have done it, that woman was sent to hospital, she died there. Regular people watched, you compromised us! What was you thinking?". Michael laughs. "Unbelievable. You are not my father and you never will be", Michael leaves the room slamming the door.

Randol's wife of twenty years, Lindsey, walks in and sees him with his hands running through his hair stressing. "Hey, he will get there", she encourages. "Somehow my dear I don't think he will", he replies going over and embracing with his wife. "The boy is just like how you used to be. Come on, they are waiting for you out there".

Lindsey and Randol enter the main living room of the Malonie mansion where the rest of the family are gathered. Henry passes Randol a glass of wine he poured in advance for him. "Here's to my brother, and to the new era of the Malonie dynasty", he declares raising his glass. Michael is stood in the corner of the room not drinking. "So what happens now in terms of the family? Who is our don?", asks Johnny. "All that will be decided in the next few days", Randol quickly responds. "It's my brother, Sal. Do not fool us", Michael pipes up. "All that will be discussed later Mikey, nobody knows right now". Michael smirks before exiting through the glass patio doors into the garden. Ralph soon follows him to calm him down, Ralph is the Jackle to Michael's Hyde.

Michael picks up a rifle that was leaning against one of the garden walls and begins to shoot empty beers bottles resting opposite. Ralph stands next to him and lowers his gun. "Whatever decision they make, seventy five percent of it would have come from your father you know", Ralph tries to warm Michael up to the idea of Salvatore's possible return. "I am next in line not him. He took his ball and left", Michael snaps. "He had no choice Mikey. You know that. Your father wanted it this way". Michael carries on shooting, knocking one bottle off hard smashing it, this makes him smile. "This family is too old fashioned, it's not the 60's anymore. It is 1982, the world has changed", he shoots another bottle. "Respect your father's instinct, he knew Sal was next in line and would one day return. You said yourself, this family needs a new direction. Sal could be the man we need. Give your brother a chance", Ralph lectures on. "You mean good Ralph. Your heart doesn't belong in this life, it will get you hurt one day. Let me do me and you do you sunshine", Michael sarcastically pats Ralph on the head before walking back inside.

Ralph has always looked out for his younger cousin ever since they were children. When Salvatore left five years ago, Ralph stepped in and filled the boots of an older brother to Michael. He always calmed his crazy antics and talked him out of doing stupid things. Ralph is Michael's unsung guardian angel.

Overseas in London England, the clock has struck 6am and the blonde haired, blue eyed Salvatore Malonie has awoken next to his beautiful girlfriend Lucy who he kisses on her forehead before making his way to work. Ever since his move to England, Salvatore has settled down and found that his main commitment is to his lover. He does miss his family but knows the move was for the best.

Salvatore works at 'Daily Dose', a modern day newspaper business where he writes up stories from around the world. Starting as a rookie, he soon worked his way up to be a respectful writer. He has become someone who the other employees go to when they are seeking advice. Salvatore has time for everyone, a friend of his will never be a burden. Salvatore is well respected in the company. This is exemplified by him having his own reserved parking spot.

Salvatore makes his way into his office which he shares with his irritating co-worker AJ. AJ is scruffily dressed and always has crisp crumbs on his tie. "Morning treacle, you should have seen the solid eight I pulled last night at Montie's man. She was wild", AJ greets his co-worker. "You still go to that shit hole?", Salvatore laughs at AJ. "We are not all tied down like you Sal", AJ remarks. "It's called love AJ, and you aint gonna find it in Monties", Salvatore sits at his desk where he loads up a rundown of stories the morning has brought. The main headlines read; Queen Street Mill Closes (the last steam driven weaving shed to work commercially), United States Put An Embargo On Libyan Oil Imports, Michael Malonie Kills Reporter In Public'. Salvatore immediately clicks on the Michael Malonie link and opens the document which contains all the information he has to write about today. As he continues to read, he finds out his father is dead. He leaves the room and dials the Malonie mansion but doesn't get an answer.

After a long day working and waiting for a phone call from his uncle, Salvatore enters his semi-detached home to a candle lit dinner made by Lucy. "Babe you shouldn't have", Lucy detects a tone of sadness in his voice and rushes over. "Before you say one more word, I have something to tell you. You're going to be a dad". Salvatore doesn't know how to respond. He drops his briefcase and cries. Today has been the best and worst day of his life. Lucy notices something isn't right, she sits him down on the couch and asks him what is wrong. Salvatore opens up and tells her about his father and what it could mean for their future.

One hour and a heated debate later, Salvatore sleeps on the couch as Lucy sleeps in her bed. It all was about to change.

The next day saw the usual routine for Salvatore, he got up early and went to work fighting the courage not to ram AJ's packet of crisp down his throat. However, for Lucy she would be called upon by an unexpected guest...

It was 11am when she was rudely interrupted from her morning read with banging on the front door. She opened it to the sight of Randol and Henry Malonie. "Good evening mam, I'm here to talk to you about your husband", Randol charms. "What's happened? Who are you?", Lucy panics a little. "Please mam, it would be best if we come in", Randol furthers. Lucy lets them.

Randol and Lucy sit in the living room and Henry stands behind the door. "What I'm about to tell you is absolutely crazy but true, Lucy we need you on our side", Randol begins to explain the whole situation to her, knowing that he needs to get Lucy on board or Salvatore will never leave England and come home.

Seven hours later Salvatore returns home with a bunch of red roses for Lucy to make amends for last night's heated argument, the first one in a year. He is greeted to the sight of Lucy handing Randol a cup of tea. "Are they for me", Randol laughs as he gets up to hug his eldest nephew. "You took your time, I had to read about it in a newspaper", a slightly pissed of Salvatore speaks. "We had a lot to do Sal, we are here now". Salvatore looks confused, "we?" he asks. The toilet upstairs flushes and down walks Henry. "I love the smell of your toilet paper. Man, I love this country", Henry comically speaks. "Henry, been a while", Salvatore greets his cousin. "Sal, I think you know why we are here", Randol directs Salvatore back to the original point. "You want to take me home?". Salvatore brushes past and stands with his girl. "I have a family now Randy, things have changed", Salvatore pledges his loyalty to his girl. "They have told me everything Sal, they want us both to go to New York", Lucy perks. Salvatore turns around to face Lucy directly, "is that something you want? New York?", he asks not wanting to make a decision about his future without her in it.

She was his lifeline, when he came to London he had nobody until he met her. They met at in a coffee shop on his second day in the country, they had been inseparable ever since. "I think it's something we need to talk about, alone", she prompts her lover to tell the gangsters to leave because she doesn't have the courage too. "Randy, give us time to think this through", Salvatore advocates. "Okay. But Sal, family is before anything. Nobody is above family. Your Dad wanted you home". "Well he had five years to bring me home", Salvatore takes insult in Randol's recent comment and snaps back rendering Randol speechless. "I'll give you twenty hours", Randol says on his way through the front door.

Meanwhile back in New York, Ralph and Michael have been sent on a job to interrogate a pub owner who has reportedly been hosting Santana family meetings in his backroom.

They enter the half empty bar with Michael spitting on the floor and stealing an old man's drink on his way past. "We are here to see Ben", the calm and collected Ralph asks the blonde, big breasted bar maid. "And maybe you later?", Michael adds, Ralph hits his arm to knock him into shape. "One sec", the bar maid goes into the back after giving a look of rejection to the unhinged Michael. Ten minutes later she returns and tells the two that Ben isn't here today, "Listen lady you don't want any trouble, we know your boss is here. If he wants his pub in one piece, he needs to see us right here right now", Ralph demands. Michael goes into his inside blazer pocket and pulls out his revolver and rests it on the bar, spinning it and pointing it at the bar maid. "Okay I'll go get him. He told me to say that", she rushes back in the back room.

Ben rushes out as the bar maid pushes him out of the back room out of fear for her own life. He falls behind the bar. "Gentlemen, what do I owe this visit?", he begins to shake in fear. "We represent the Malonie family. Its best if we use that backroom, you don't want your customers to see you cry, do you?", Ralph uses the charm he inherited from his father on the weak pig-headed man.

Ben, trembling in fear, escorts them through to the backroom where they stand near a pool table. Michael picks up a pool que and smacks it down on the side table, splitting it in two. Ralph sits at a nearby table, they are playing 'good cop, bad cop'. "One word out of line and this goes up your arse", Michael says getting right in Ben's ugly face. "He's not joking, I've seen him do it", Ralph enforces the fear. "Mr Benzino, do you know why we might be here?", a calm Ralph asks. "No sir, I have great respect for your family". "Michael", Ralph signals his cousin. Michael circles the man like a lion teasing his pray before jabbing him in the eye with the cut end of the que. The man begins to piss himself. "Mr Benzino, do you know why we might be here", Ralph asks again. "I'm sorry. Yes I do but they didn't give me a choice", the man cries. "Now we are on a level", Ralph speaks. "Now what we are going to do is stop this", Michael adds. "Please don't kill me I have a little girl", Ben begs. "Don't beg Mr Benzino don't belittle yourself like that. On behalf of Randol Malonie, we are now buying your pub from you. You have no say in this unless you want to be found hung from your bedroom by your little girl. You will ask for five thousand, but we will give you two thousand", Ralph informs the man. "And you'll fucking like it", Michael adds. Ralph pulls a cheque out of his pocket and places it in the pocket of the man's pissed up jeans. "Pleasure doing business with you, Mr Benzino", Ralph pats him on the side of his cheek and the two leave after a successful meeting.

Back in London, Salvatore and Lucy are deciding what their next move will be, do they stay, or do they go? Lucy is intrigued by the mafia and suddenly finds herself more attracted to Salvatore now the mafia past has come to light. She always wanted to go to America too, for her it was a win win. In regards to Salvatore, he knows he upset a lot of people by not siding against father when he 'walked out' of the family. His relationship with his brother in particular had worsened, they haven't spoken in five years. Moving back home would be a big gamble for him, let alone running the family. This would take more than a night's sleep too weigh into proportion.

The next day came and Lucy walked downstairs into the living room to find Salvatore sat on his chair thinking deeply, having not slept at all the previous night. She holds his hand. "Let's do it. Your family needs you and growing up with a big family with all the protection will help us loads with our little one", she softly says to her tired boyfriend pointing down at her soon to inflate stomach. They decide to go to America. A couple of hours of packing later, they meet Randol and Henry at the airport to their delight and travel to New York.

3,459 miles away, Johnny Malonie receives a phone call from a mysterious caller asking to meet up at Rico's Dinner in Times Square. "On whose behalf does this concern?", Johnny asks the caller. "On behalf of Serbeano Malonie. Rico's Dinner, thirty minutes. Come alone", the caller hangs up. Johnny doesn't know if he is walking into his own coffin but is so intrigued he collars a taxi and embarks down to the most famous square in the world.

Rico's dinner is a small, midget building that is truly like the needle in the giant haystack of times square. Forty years on the square, Rico Angelo started the coffee shop after the second world war, and it manages to run smoothly year after year. It is a small treasure in the ever changing and modernising times square chest.

Johnny Malonie sits at a table in the dinner awaiting his mystery caller, he orders an iced tea while he waits. He keeps checking his watch in anticipation. He looks around the dinner looking to see if he has just walked right into a hit job. He sees regular New Yorkers, old couples with their grandchildren, businessmen and women on their lunch breaks, he wasn't going to get hit here. As far he thought, he was safe.

Twenty minutes late, a tall blonde-haired man walks in and sits opposite the on edge Johnny. The smoothly dressed man has a well-trimmed beard, and scarred eyes that look like they have lived through a few wars and seen some damaging events. "You're twenty minutes late, that's an insult", Johnny declares. "I wanted to make sure you came Mr Malonie. My name is Hunter I work on behalf of Santino Rully, he has an opportunity for you", the man informs. "I don't do business with Rully", Johnny stands. Hunter holds up a gun underneath his overcoat pointing at Johnny. "How do I not know that's just your finger", Johnny, only seeing a point in the overcoat, says. "Do you really want to keep standing to find out?", Hunter remarks making Johnny sit back down.

"Don't be so rude Malonie, my boss likes you. He likes you more than he likes the rest of your lot. You see, he is very psychological, he sees something in you that Serbeano or Randy never did. He sees the fire in you. You're not used there in your own family, you're just an after thought to them. They don't care about you, why would they allow you to come here alone if they did?", Hunter, planting the seed of betrayal in Johnny's head, preaches. "What does Razor's son want with me?".

A waitress comes over to take Hunter's order. He orders a tuna pasty, much to the distain of Johnny and the waitress. "You need to ask is what do you need from Santino? Santino wants your brains, he wants your potential. He wants you to give us the names of the police on your payroll, and in return he will give you the Gumbini crime family", Hunter offers. "Joey

Gumbini would never allow that", Johnny says. "Santino is going to whack Joey, he just needs a 'poster boy', Joey is over that hill", the waitress returns armed with the disgusting tuna pasty. "No hesitation, this isn't the time for doubt. Your either with us or beneath us swimming in the home of this delicious tuna", Hunter threatens. "I have always wanted to run an organisation of my own. Just the names that's all he wants? My family won't know it was me?", Johnny enquires. "No one will ever know we met in this dinner today", Hunter smiles knowing he has won the cousin of Serbeano Malonie. The two shake hands on the deal.

Did Johnny Malonie just make a deal with the Devil? Will it be worth betraying his blood like that? What consequences will he face if they ever find out what he did here today?

Four hours later, the family are all gathered in the main living room where they are anticipating the return of the rightful heir to the Malonie throne, Salvatore Malonie. Martha is so excited to see her son, however, this is not the first time she has seen him in the five years as she sneakily met up with him a few times travelling to London. Michael is drunk as he started drinking with Moxie throughout the day, it was his way of preparing himself for the reunion with his brother. Ralph quickly sprayed the two with aftershave to dilute the smell of booze.

Randol entered the living room with his entourage of Salvatore, Lucy, and Henry. The family cheered as Martha runs over and hugged her son so tight. "It's good to see everyone, ah this is my girl, Lucy", Salvatore greeted his family and introduced them to his love. Sull played the stereo and the homecoming began. Salvatore and Lucy went around the room talking to the family members. Michael had his eyes locked on his brother as he went round the room.

Ralph looked over at his younger cousin and saw the rage in his eyes, he went over and patted him on the back. "Mikey now is not the time. Smile and shake your brother's hand", Ralph trying to put out the fire before it even starts speaks softly in Michael's ear. Michael takes one ungraceful gulp of his red wine and leaves the room. Salvatore looks up and sees this and follows his brother out of the room. Ralph stands next to his brother, Moxie. "What's his problem now?", Ralph asks his slightly intoxicated younger brother. "He should be Don not Sal. Five fucking years now he shows up like a celebrity. He is nothing". It doesn't take a scientist to realise that Moxie is drunk so Ralph lets his comments slide.

Salvatore finds Michael in the kitchen opening another beer, using the sharp edge of the counter as a substitute to a bottle opener. "Brother, it's good to see you", Salvatore opens his arms for a brotherly hug but Michael stares at him coldly. "You aren't a brother of mine", Michael shoulder barges past his brother.

Within two hours the press had already reported Salvatore's return as they had been tipped off at the airport and followed the entourage in the shadows as Henry drove Salvatore back to the mansion. The world now knows that Salvatore was back and it didn't take a genius to work out that he would soon be the new Don Malonie.

In the upcoming weeks, Randol paired Salvatore with Sull to reinforce his training with revolvers as it had been five years since he even held one let alone shot one. Sull became his mentor when it came to the physical side of the family business. Randol, on the other hand, was teaching Salvatore all he needed to know to handle the business side of things. Four gruelling weeks of them sculpting their future don and head of the family. It wasn't easy and at times Salvatore regretted returning, he had never worked harder in his life. But it was his beautiful girl, Lucy, who kept him going. Each time he fell into a groove of dullness and regret she was there to pick him up and rewire his circuits. Behind every great man is an even greater woman.

The spring leaves fell as they entered April. Salvatore was almost finished his process of learning what it takes to be head of the table. Randol was taking him to a meeting with a detective on their payroll, Josh Sutcliffe. Randol had been taking Salvatore to make him watch and learn the negotiation and handling of meetings process that plagued the esteemed title of Don. Josh, like them, was an Irish American and had been on the Malonie payroll ever since 1975.

Randol and Salvatore wait in Josh's office. "I'm going to sit but you stand", Randol orders. He wants Salvatore to stand to show a sign of attitude, he feels if they both sit, the detective might feel he is on their level, whereas, if one stands it shows aggression and means Josh won't take advantage because they are indeed above him.

Josh enters the room and shakes both men's hands. "Gentlemen, I asked you for this meeting because we have a problem. Two weeks ago a Mr Taylor was found deceased in his flat, now this man was a weapons smuggler who stole shipments from you, but he was also the nephew of my superior. He wants to reopen the investigation", the detective informs. "We had no involvement in that crime", Randol quickly averts. "The thing is Mr Malonie, the car belonging to Sull Malonie was spotted and photographed by Taylor's neighbour Mr Shabani. He intends to use the photo and show the Chief", the detective hates breaking bad news to the Malonies, he always fears his head will be found in a garbage bin. "I see, this is a problem then. I appreciate you warning us detective. We will pay Mr Shabini a visit", Randol slides over a fifty-dollar bill to Josh who quickly sneaks it into his blazer pocket. Randol stands and shakes Josh's hand before leaving.

Back in the car Randol questions what happened two weeks ago when Sull took Salvatore on a job visiting Mr Taylor. Salvatore explains...

Sull was driving him and Salvatore down Houston Street where they would pay a visit to Mr Taylor, who was a weapon smuggler working on behalf of the Malonies. They had found out that Taylor was stealing weapons off their cargos and selling them on the black market instead of shipping them to Saudi Arabia, Australia, and Japan. Randol sent Sull and Salvatore to beat Taylor, fire him, and get the money he owes from the stolen goods, he specifically ordered them not to kill him, he didn't want any more unnecessary attention on the family in the transition of mourning Serbeano and naming a new Don.

Sull and Salvatore parked up outside an old rundown apartment block and made their way into the building. They stood outside of number 14. Sull pulls out his revolver, "you stand behind me kid, it could get messy in here". Salvatore looked at Sull confused he thought this was unnecessary. "No killing, that was the order Sull, just intimidate". Sull shakes his head at Salvatore. "Kid, this gun is a guardian angel. That is how you need to see it, would you rather be dead?",

Sull asks before knocking twice hard on the door. "Room service babycakes", Sull kicks in the door and the two enter.

The flat stank. The smell of weed infected the air, curtains were drawn yet it was mid-day. Clothes all over the floor. The place was a mess. The place was more of a pit than a home.

Salvatore pulled his face as the smell raped him. Sull finds the man in his living room in mid blow job from a street tart prostitute. Taylor panics and pushes the prostitute off at the sight of Sull. "I hope he's paying you double time love", Sull remarks as he points his revolver at Taylor's head. The prostitute is infested in fear and runs out of the flat. "Afternoon grifter you've been a naughty boy", Sull says as he smacks Taylor with the end of his gun. He then drags him off the couch and into the kitchen where pulls out a butcher knife at him. "Sal, tell him why we are here?", Sull directs Salvatore. "Mr Taylor, we have it on good authority that you have been stealing from our family", an uncomfortable Salvatore says. This was his first job after all. "Come on Sal, make him fear you", Sull throws the butcher knife Sal's way as he pins Taylor down on the chopping board. Salvatore stabs the knife down on the board next to his head. "TELL US WHY!?!", Salvatore shouts in an attempt to be more intimidating. Taylor reaches over and grabs the knife, he slashes Sull's left arm sending him back in pain, he shoves Salvatore out of the way and makes a run for it.

Salvatore trips him and before he can do another thing, Sull rages in and takes the clock off the wall before redecorating Taylor's head with it. Taylor falls to his carpet with a wounded head with the clock now around his neck. "Man, I love this job", Sull finds delight in his infliction of pain.

"I got a better price than you pigs ever gave me", Taylor spits out as he crawls away slowly. Sull stands on his feet stalling him. "Say it again darling?". Salvatore is uncomfortable and just wants Sull to leave it. "Let's just get the money he owes and leave", Salvatore pledges. "Where can we find the money", Sull asks Taylor. "Up your fat arse", Taylor responds. Sull presses down on his foot crushing it. "Where can we find the money you owe us, you cheap ass slut?". "Under my bed in a safe", Taylor wrestles out of his mouth in pain. Salvatore goes into the bedroom to get it. "We need a code for a safe, smart ass", Sull wants the code. "3214", Taylor shouts to Sal.

Sull notices that professional wrestling is on Taylor's TV. "Look at the size of that Haystack", Sull reaches over and pulls Taylor's hair, lifting him to catch the wrestling match. Salvatore re-enters the room with a handful of cash, "its only half". "That's all I have. You can't get anything else", Taylor panicked remembering he wasted it all at the casino two weekends ago. "No because you were seen in the casino across the road the other week, you really are lower than low", Sull spits on the back of Taylor's head. "Fuck you Malonies! You cheat, you lie, you steal. Your all fucking wrong, I hope them Italians wipe the floor with you all", Taylor rages. Sull has had enough, he quickly pulls out his gun with the silencer on and shoots Taylor dead in the back of the head.

Salvatore pulls Sull off the body of the obnoxious Mr Taylor. "What have you done? We were told not to kill!", an irritated Salvatore rants. "Calm it grifter, noting is going to happen, this punk was a nobody look around you", Sull has no remorse he feels the world is a better place with this jackass gone.

Randol was extremely annoyed as he didn't know that Taylor was killed. However, it was too late now to go mad they have to play with what was dealt. In response to Sutcliffe's warning, Randol soon sends Sull and Henry to deal with Shabini and to stop him from ratting on the family. To do this, Sull and Henry track down one of Shabini's oldest friends, Erik Romonov. They murder Erik and send his right foot to Shabini's door in a package. From this, Shabini knew he had to keep his mouth shut and he instantly destroyed the photos he had and then soon moved to Chicago.

As the transition for Salvatore from man to Don was under way, Johnny Malonie had begun a transition of his own. A transition of deceit. He had sent a list of names of police officers and detectives under the Malonie family payroll to Hunter and Santino Rully. In return they had invited him to their privately owned nightclub, 'Electric City', the city's first and only 24 hour club, tonight to take business further. He was instructed to enter via the back to avoid been seen.

It was 11am and Johnny Malonie entered the nightclub, he was instantly greeted by a thin brunette waitress who handed him a gin and tonic before escorting him into what was a stripper's booth. He was getting ready for his stripper, he smelt his breathe and tweaked his hair as well as beginning to un-tie his belt even though there was a strict 'no touching' policy, but he was a Malonie, he didn't care.

Hunter and Santino entered to his disappointment. He quickly fastened his belt back up. "Sorry to disappoint your Johnny John", Hunter laughed. He introduced him to Santino. Santino was a slick black-haired man who was known for his well-dressed nature. People knew Santino more for his wealth rather than the crimes he committed.

The two shake hands. "I wanted to thank you personally for the list of names you delivered for us, it mustn't have been easy betraying your family",

Santino thanked Johnny. "It's for the best". "I admire that", Santino made Johnny feel comfortable and welcome. Santino moves closer to Johnny and grabs his hand, "I want you to know that whatever happens next is purely business and not personal. Your family have wronged mine", Santino preached. Johnny moves in close to Santino, "you do what you gotta do", Johnny and Santino clink drinks. "Tomorrow we take out Gumbini and that family becomes yours", Santino informs his brand new lap dog.

The three men party and see the night out together celebrating their new relationship. Little to their knowledge Serbeano Malonie had hired a bar maid to work in that club to always keep an eye on Rully's movements. This was the last act he did before he passed. She saw everything. Within two hours she had called Randol and told him of Johnny's act of betrayal...

Twelve hours later, Randol had called Johnny into Serbeano's office. He had Salvatore in attendance to pick up things and learn. He sat at his brother's desk and had Salvatore stood behind him. As soon as Johnny sits opposite him, Randol stands and pours himself a whisky from the drinking shelf in the office. "Gumbini was killed this morning in a 'car accident', that's how I know what the girl on the phone told me was true", Randol looks into Johnny's faulty confused eyes. "That's a shame, he was a great man", Johnny commented. "He was, wasn't he? Apparently a child ran across the road and he swerved and crashed. I don't buy it though", Randol looks into Johnny's eyes the whole time as he sits back down. "Well accidents happen Randy". Randol knows from Johnny's eyes that he is lying. Johnny's eyes are flicking constantly around the room avoiding eye contact with Randol for more than two minutes. "They do Johnny, they do. Show me your tongue", he asks. Johnny refuses so Randol orders Salvatore to force Johnny's mouth open, so he does. His tongue is blue. Randol knows that 'Electric City' is known for selling drinks that turn your tongue blue.

Randol opens the desk and pulls up a revolver with a silencer on and shoots Johnny in his leg. Johnny collapses onto the floor. "I know everything Johnny. You sold us out to Rully's boy!", Randol shouts as Salvatore stands in shock. "I had an associate working in that club last night, I know everything. If you weren't family, I would kill you. Get up!", Randol shouts orders. Johnny uses his surroundings to pick his lying, backstabbing body up. "I have booked you and your wife on one-way tickets to New Orleans. You will live, and stay there. As of this moment you are no longer in the family", Randol puts away his gun and slides an envelope with two one-way tickets to New Orleans in over to him. Randol then necks his drink.

Randol let the family know what Johnny had done and within the day he was gone, presumably to New Orleans.

"You should have killed him", Salvatore says to Randol. "I don't kill blood, no matter what they have done", Randol preached. "But he put your life and our lives at risk. He broke that rule when he sold us out, he is scum", Salvatore gave his take on the betrayal of Johnny Malonie. "Listen, it's my way. No one who shares our blood will be killed by our blood", Randol, defended himself, responds. "He is out there still walking free, he's just going to get worse. You have given him the greenlight to get us", Salvatore disagrees with his uncle's strategy and feels Johnny was best dead, now he is still alive he might continue his work with Rully. Nothing was stopping his return for vengeance. "Any man who can lie, cheat, or hurt their family isn't a man at all", Salvatore heroically says as he leaves the office.

Later that night, Salvatore visited the local Church to his father's tombstone. He kneeled in front of it. "Ey pops, what did you bring me into? I hope I make you proud, a lot of things have got to change though, we need to adapt and modernise", he says. From the distance a lone gunman observes from the trees behind. He slowly creeps out sneaking up on Sal. Salvatore manages to get his sights on the man as he can see the outlie of his figure through a glass vase on the grave. The man gets closer. The cold nose of the gun presses on the back of his head. "Salvatore Malonie, say hello to the devil", before the man shoots, Salvatore spins around and tackles him down.

The man drops his gun. The two wrestle. The man kicks Salvatore into a nearby tombstone, he then spears him through it. Salvatore spins around in absolute agony matched with pure pain, and mounts the man delivering five shots in his skull. The man grabs a rock close by and smacks Salvatore in the head knocking him off.

The cowardness fuelled gunman then goes to get his gun. Salvatore sees this and jumps up chasing the man and tackling him down, he reaches for the gun and shoots the man through in his right ear sending the bullet straight to his brain killing him. This is Salvatore's first kill.

Immense guilt filled Salvatore, even though he knows that this man was sent to kill him he still feels 'dirty' for killing him. He went straight to Randol when he came back and told him he doesn't think that this life was for him. Randol slaps him hard across his face. "This life is all you have. You are fighting in a war", an insulted Randol rants. "I am not a soldier!", Salvatore passionately exclaims. Randol goes into his cabinet and pulls out a revolver that belonged to his brother upon hearing this. "Kiddo we are all soldiers. This is business don't get too caught up in the messy things, you either adapt or perish. Don't bring shame to this family. Take this", Randol hands Salvatore the revolver. "Never look the man in his eyes, it will confuse your judgment. Look at his forehead, that's my trick. That was your father's, hold and use it with pride or God help you so. You are the future of this family", Randol holds Salvatore's cheek.

After the talk, Salvatore finds his wife in her bedroom combing her vibrant hair. He goes over and kisses her forehead. "What have we become Lucy?". Lucy puts the comb down and holds her boyfriend. She knows Salvatore isn't handling this transition well. "We have become what we needed to be, your family needs you to be the man of tomorrow not the man of today. You need to put them first and protect them at all costs, we both know that if your father would have lived ten more years this family would have fallen. You need to be the Don to bring about change. Who do you want to be, the follower who is seen as a sheep, or the leader who is respected by all", these words from Lucy inspire Salvatore and enable him to now know what he has to do.

The clock hits 1am, the annoying sound of a phone call rudely disturbs Ralph and Michael who are sat in the living room drinking wine discussing movements of the Santana family. Ralph picks up the phone, its Ben from the pub. He is reporting that two customers are causing trouble and he needs back up force to handle the situation. Ralph turns to Michael and tells him the situation, "you going to tag along?", Ralph asks his younger cousin. "Nah. You can handle two drunk idiots", Michael goes off to bed leaving Ralph to drive down to the pub alone.

Upon entry, Ralph notices that the pub is stone cold silent and empty. Something is wrong. From out of nowhere a Santana family hitman jumps up from behind the bar and opens fire with a tommy gun. Ralph has no time to pull his own gun up, he is relentlessly murdered and left in a pool of his own blood.

Two hours later the family are called by one of the officers on their payroll to inform them on the news. The broken family are faced with more cracks.

They are all gathered in the morning, Randol is sat with his wife on the couch in complete bits. Salvatore looks around the room and sees his broken family. He knows he has to step up. "I say we burn that pub down and declare war on these Italian fucks", Michael breaks the eerie silence. "They need to be shot", he furthers. "Stop Michael", Randol softly speaks. "Bring them hear and cut off a bit of skin each day, torture the immigrant pigs", Michael has hate in his face, he is spitting his words out. "MICHAEL STOP! SHUT UP! For once!", Randol snaps in fury. Salvatore sees this as his opportunity to step up. "We need to find Ben, get what we need to know then kill him. We then call a meeting of the five families, we can't take Santana out without their permission or another war will break. We then, with their permission, move on Santana", this shocks the family as no one expected Salvatore to come out with a plan so fast. "With your approval Randy, I would like to set up that meeting for tomorrow. Whilst I do that, I want Sull and Henry to track down Ben. Mother call Alexa, we need our family together now more than ever. Michael and Moxie stay in the house at all times for now we can't risk anything else. That goes for everyone else, this family is under complete lockdown", Salvatore orders. Randol gives his approval. They get to work.

April 22$^{nd}$. The meeting of the five families. The five families consist of New York's most powerful families; Malonie, Seigel, Hurst, Kelly, and Sutcliffe. Each family runs their own area of the city and when monumental decisions such as an assignation or a breakout of a potential war happens, it needs the approval of the families to prevent a war from within the families.

The five families were formed in 1931, after Marlon Kelly won the war between the Gumbini family. This war was taken to the streets and even had civilians killed. The union of the families were formed to prevent a war like this from ever breaking out again. It was the bloodiest war in the New York's history with an astonishing total of 500 casualties. The Malonies were admitted to the five families in 1962 after their rise.

The meetings always take place in the town hall. Salvatore and Randol are representing the Malonies', a fat bearded Tony Siegel and his consigliere, Brady, represent the Siegel family, James Hurst and Donald represent the Hurst family, Stephen Kelly and Kevin represent the Kellys', and Mark Sutcliffe and Chris represent the Sutcliffes'.

They all sit on a long ominous table, each with their own reserved seats. The room is dark with no windows for extra security. This was enforced in 1979 after an assignation attempt on the Kellys'. They usually only meet once a year. However, an emergency meeting can be called in a case that requires urgent attention.

This is Salvatore's first meeting, and he is sat extremely nervous but he knows it is necessary. Sometimes no matter how you feel, the most uncomfortable things are the most rewarding.

Randol stands to introduce his nephew, "Thank you gentlemen for accepting this meeting today. This meeting will be conducted by my nephew and future Don, Salvatore Malonie", Randol sits and hands the meeting over to Salvatore. "Thank you gentlemen for accepting this meeting with such short notice. I called you hear today to ask permission from you all to take out a killing. I wish to kill Roman Santana and end the three-decade war between his family and mine", the rest of the families are sat back in shock.

After a few minutes of pure silence, Tony Seigel chimes in, "Do you realise what you are getting yourself into? Roman Santana is a close ally of mine, he is responsible for 15% of my income", Seigel disapproves. "I understand, that is why I propose once the killing is done, the Malonie family will invest and make up for that 15%", Salvatore has thought this through and done his research. "I also disapprove", Stephen Kelly adds, "Roman Santana is one of the most dangerous men out there, I don't wish to make him an enemy of mine by approving your request. I think your family has fallen if you ask me. Serbeano would never be this crazy", he further develops his reasoning. "With all due respect Mr Kelly, my father was at war with Santana for thirty years, he wanted him dead as much as I did", Salvatore fired back. "Yes, but he would never come out point blank and ask us to give permission, he would deal with him on his own", Kevin, who was sat with Stephen, defends. "Again, with all due respect Mr Kevin Kelly, my father did deal with him his own way and that's why Roman Santana still walks these streets, and you all won't admit it but that's why he still has you all by his strings. You're his puppets, you all fear Santana and I don't. What do I need to do get your permission?", Salvatore shows his passionate energy. "You don't", James Hurst says. "Then I hereby withdraw the Malonie family from union of the five families", Salvatore announces to the table.

The table outrages. "And do you stand by this decision Randol?", Mark Sutcliffe asks. Randol takes one look at his nephew and sees something in his eyes he hasn't seen before, the same fresh look that his father once showed in his early days of being Don. The look of fresh passion and fire, it was a beautiful thing. "I do", Randol says as him and Salvatore get up to leave.

As soon as the meeting had concluded Stephen Kelly had phoned the Santana family to inform them of Salvatore's upcoming blooded intentions.

The car ride back was tense. Randol only sided with Salvatore in the meeting to show a united front, Serbeano always said the weakness of a team is shown through division, unity is the most powerful strategy. "There is no way we can take down Santana alone, what were you thinking in there!", Randol yells at his nephew. "We will. Have trust in me Randy I promise you, Santana will pay for killing Ralph", Salvatore defends. "It's crazy! Do you have anyone we can call in to help? Us alone won't be enough", Randol enquires fearing the future of the family. "When I was in London there were two famous twin brothers who ran the show down there, I became friends with them", Salvatore replied much to Randol's delight. "Are they coming up?", Randol asked quickly. "They are in business with Kelly, so they won't help us", Salvatore broke the news to

Randol. "Well fuck me Sal what have you done?", Randol worries. "Trust me uncle, I have a plan".

As this was happening, Sull and Henry had found out that Ben was set to attend a rally against nuclear weapons in New York's Central Park, this is where they would take him out.

In terms of the family's reaction to Salvatore pulling out of the five families, it was polarising. Michael hated it and believed Sal had betrayed all that their father had stood for, this worsened their already damaged relationship. Martha, Randol, and Lindsey stood by Salvatore to show a united front.

Michael had a few beers coming as the result of mourning Ralph, his voice of reason was now no more. He wanted a one-on-one meeting with his brother and managed to find him alone in the garden. "I feel they are all against me", Salvatore said referring to his family's reaction to his recent call of judgement. "They are and they should be. Who do you think you are?", a drunken Michael blurts. "I'm not here to fight Michael. Now is not the time", Salvatore, wanting to diffuse the situation speaks. "Five years. Five years I waited for you. And now you are here I don't know what I want to do", Michael tenses his fist. "Sober up would be one idea", Salvatore smirks. "You come home to a hero's welcome and suddenly you're the man. Well I won't listen to you, I know for sure Moxie won't", Michael says as Salvatore stands to leave the conversation. Michael smashes his bottle of beer down on the patio in a rage.

The five o'clock news aired, and it immediately caught the attention of Randol and Martha. "It is believed that Detective Parker was found head down on his desk after drinking a drink containing Botulinum toxin. Police at this time don't believe this was a suicide as the letter 'R' was found freshly carved into his leg. At this time it is hard to say who is responsible, but one thing for sure is, the killer is out on the lose", the reporter sternly said.

Randol brushes his hands through his hair in stress, he knows who is responsible. "Detective Parker was on our payroll, Santino Rully has the list of names. Razor is back", Randol, stood like he has just seen a ghost, claims. Floods of Arty's murder hit him;

June 18th 1976. Arty and Randol had been sent to scout out a possible location of the hiding Razor Rully. They had been informed by a close ally that Rully was seen in a lighthouse overlooking Brighton Beach. They drove down to one of the city's most populated beaches. The beach was rammed with citizens on this not so sunny Saturday night. It was mainly full of teenagers having BBQs and drinking illegally. The two brothers calmly walk the pier to the lighthouse.

"What's your plan?", Arty asks his brother. "We go in and set the smoke bombs off. We smoke him to the top and deal with him at the top of the house, we can get rid of the body easy that way", Randol lays out his plan. "Throw him from the top?", Arty double checks. "The rocks at the bottom of the pier will sort him out", Randol informs.

The two brothers breach the bottom door of the lighthouse and throw down their smoke bombs which soon blind the environment. "Now", Randol and Arty open fire on the bottom floor to intimidate. They see Rully on the steps leading to the top. Their plan is working.

300 steps later, the brothers have forced Razor Rully on the top of the pier on the outside balcony. Rully isn't outnumbered though, he got tipped off. On the pier with him stands Hunter, his close associate. Hunter is armed with a tommy gun. The brothers storm through the top door and are met by the two thugs. We have a tag team turmoil stand-off. "Looks like we have ourselves in a little western here gentlemen", Rully remarks. Randol soon realises that they were set up into a trap.

Thunder hits the sky as a storm breaks through. Randol has one last smoke bomb left, he grabs it from his blazer pocket and smashes it rendering everyone's eyes ineffective. Shots go off but nobody is hit. Randol urges himself onto Hunter and the two brawl. Arty does the same to Razor. Razor was a former professional street fighter, he had Arty's number. Razor hurdles Arty against the side of the balcony barrier which overlooks the hard rocks at the bottom of the pier.

Razor spits in Arty's face before punching him repeatedly and violently in his stomach. Arty is losing his breath the punches are that firm and rock solid. Rully grabs Art's helpless face before he realises the rocks they are standing above. He kisses his once ally and friend before grabbing his feet and throwing him over the balcony killing him on instant impact on the rocks. Randol sees this and falls to the ground in shock. Rully and Hunter beat Randol unconscious before sending him back to the Malonie mansion, keeping him alive as a warning to the rest of the family.

The 'ally' that tipped the family off on Rully's location was the one who set the family up. Within ten hours after Arty's death, Randol and Sull had tracked down the man and had taken him into a forest with a potato bag on his head.

Sull strikes the man with a crowbar crippling him to his knees. Randol, with his face still heavily wounded and bruised from the Rully attack, pulls out his revolver. "Ivar, have you ever heard the story about the lion who befriended the Zebra?", the man fails to answer. Randol looks up at Sull which gives him the signal to hit him again with the crowbar. "Have you?", Randol asks again. "No", the man coughs up. "Well one day the lion puts his trusts in a zebra, a zebra he has known for years. He trusted the zebra. One day though, the zebra ate the lion's lunch and betrayed him. This shocked the lion, broke his heart. He knew though he now had to eat the zebra. Suddenly he didn't feel so bad though, because he knew that he was always meant to eat the zebra", Randol kneels down and yanks the man's head up. "We are the fucking lions Ivar", Randol steps back and shoots the man in the back of the head dead.

Randol rushes over to Salvatore to tell him about Rully's return, who is talking to Sull and Henry in Serbeano's office. Randol asks to talk in private, so Sull and Henry leave. "I think we might have made a mistake pulling out of the families so soon. Razor is in the city!", Randol breaks it to Salvatore. "I know. I saw the news, but you got to see this through Randy, we take out Santana and Razor on our own backs we become the most powerful family in the city", Salvatore stands by his decision. "We could have done with the support of the families, Razor Rully isn't a man to mess with. This is a guy who once hijacked a US military Jet from the sky! He has no boundaries and will stop at nothing to have you killed", Randol doesn't feel Salvatore is fully understanding the magnitude of Rully and all that monster is capable of. "And I will be ready. We knew this day was coming. You have to trust me Randy, I'm not crazy. Things need to change with how this family handles business", Salvatore fires back, throwing shade at how Randol and Serebeano used to handle business. "I hope you know what you're doing kid, if this fails you risk every life in this house today", Randol leaves them words lingering in Sal's head.

**New York Central Park.** The day had come for **Ben** to meet his maker. Sull and Henry arrived at the sight of one million people all fighting against nuclear weapons and for the end of the current cold war. This was the largest anti-nuclear protest, and largest political demonstration in American history. With people even filling out to Fifth Avenue and Central Park West. It really was like looking for a needle in a never-ending haystack.

They knew diving into the crowd of angry, passionate, and determined people would result in a failed mission. They had discussed a plan with Salvatore to locate Ben's car and plant a bomb underneath. This should be easy, he drove a silver van everywhere he went and it had a huge dint in the roof. They believed he started living in it to prevent the Malonie and Santana families from finding him.

Within minutes they had located the van on the outskirts of the park, this should be easy. Henry was carrying the sticky bomb in a brown briefcase, all they had to do was walk around two miles to get to the makeshift house for a coward on wheels.

Sull needed to cause a distraction to get people's attention averted so Henry could plant the bomb under the van. To do this, he ran over to the other side of the road and hurdled himself onto the bonnet of an upcoming car, this worked, and Henry was able to plant the bomb by sliding the briefcase under the vehicle.

Two hours later the bomb had gone off, killing Ben and only injuring a handful of other people. This was caught live on the news as they were reporting on the protest. This was Sal's plan as he wanted the Santana's and the five families to see.

They saw alright.

Back in 10,000 square foot Malonie mansion, Salvatore enters the basement where he finds his brother and Moxie. Moxie is playing pool and Michael is sat with a beer in arm. Salvatore asks Moxie to leave so he can have a private conversation with Michael. He obliges.

"I think we need to get this sorted Mikey", Salvatore wants to finally amend the damage. "Michael. You call me Michael. I have nothing to say to you", Michael harshly comments. "Michael, for the family's sake". This comment irritates Michael who stands and gets in his brother's face. "Family? The fuck do you know about family? You don't care about us. You took your pissant ball and left for another country. We used to be close, play football together, play video games in the living room, went out drinking. Now. Well now all you are to me is a suit and tie sunshine", Michael is spitting with rage. He finds himself getting too heated so he goes over to the pool table to calm down. He plays against himself.

"It was part of pop's plan, I had no say", Salvatore tries to educate. Michael pots a snooker ball before getting back in his brother's face. "There is always a choice". Salvatore is hurt and doesn't want to continue this confrontation. He wants to just go back to his father's office and let time heal the wound. He decides to stay and get this sorted today. "I don't think you believe any of that shit you've just said. I think this all boils down to me being chosen and not you. You couldn't handle being second place, even as kids you would always cheat to win and when that didn't happen you cried like a bitch", Salvatore is getting increasingly more furious. Michael spits on the floor. "You aren't meant for this life. I had my first kill at eighteen! It should be me as Don, you're unfit. Everyone believes it, it's just that I have the balls to say it!", Michael snaps. "Unfit? You'll see. You'll all fucking see! I will be the reason this family survives what's coming, not you, not Randol, not Moxie, but me", Salvatore decides to leave before it gets physical.

Michael was always the one who was more involved with the family from a young age. At eighteen he was tagging along on jobs with Randol and Arty. One job, the day he got his first kill, changed him forever. May 4th 1966. Henry had drove Randol, Arty, and Michael down to 'Rita's Jewellery' store to kidnap the owner, Mr McHay and kill him. McHay had threatened a lawsuit against the Malonie's weapons factory after they fired his nephew for taking cocaine on the conveyor belts. The Malonies paid McHay for his silence, which at first worked. However, after McHay became broke he was suing the family again.

The actual kidnapping was hassle free; Arty disguised himself as a delivery man who called Mchay out to the back of the building to 'check off a delivery'. From here, Randol and Michael gagged McHay and put him in a bin bag head to toe, they then threw him in the boot of the car. Arty took this time to raid the store and populate a bin bag full of the jewellery. Henry then drove them to Golden Oak Forest.

All four men gathered around the boot which Randol opened revealing the two full bin bags. Randol picks up the bag on the left and places it at the end of a steep edge overlooking a tragically high drop in the forest. At the bottom of the drop was several rocks and trees. This drop would kill anyone who fell, it was thirty feet deep. "Mikey, go kick it down. It's the jewellery", Randol orders. "The jewellery? Why? We could make millions from that?", a curious young

Michael asks. "We don't need it. It's what we do, he ain't going to need it again", Arty says looking down at the other bin bag. "It's a message to our enemies. After we do jobs like this we always raid the location and scatter the goods. It's our thing. When people see the crime scene they know it's us", Randol informs. "It sends a warning", Arty develops. Michael runs over and kicks the bag off the edge sending it down thirty tortious feet.

Arty opens the other bag and pulls out a $57,000 worth watch and throws it to Michael. "Well done kid, your first kill", he says. "What? You said it was the jewellery", a shocked Michael declares as a trinkle of guilt flows through his veins. "You would have never kicked it if you knew it was McHay", Randol adds closing the boot.

Back to the present day. Alexa Malonie returned home to live with her family. Salvatore was behind this move as he wanted his family together to lower the threat of another one of his loved ones getting killed. It was mid-afternoon when she was picked up and brought back to the Malonie mansion by Henry. Alexa was light blonde and was one of the nicest girls you would ever meet. She was always warm-hearted and brought much joy to everyone she met. She arrived with her boyfriend, Shaun, a tall and tanned man who was very arrogant.

Alexa and Shaun had met on a holiday in Jamica two years ago. They both originally only wanted a one-night stand after a few cheap pints at the hotel bar. However, they both soon caught feelings after Shaun had saved Alexa's life after she nearly drowned. Weirdly enough this exact moment was when Shaun claims he fell in love with her. Only Martha and Serbeano had met Shaun once before, nobody in the family had even seen what he likes prior to today. From the stories of Shaun's troubled upbringing in San Andreas, the family wasn't too certain if they could trust him. The only reason they did is because Alexa had never been so happy. She was never too lucky with love.

Alexa and Shaun entered to the embrace of Martha, Lindsey, Lucy and Sull, Randol and Salvatore was sorting business with Moxie and Michael in Serbeano's office. Sull shook Shaun's hand as the girls hugged Alexa. "I've heard a lot about you Henry", Shaun said confidently. "I'm Sull, that's Henry", Sull pointed at his younger brother. "I knew that. How long is it before I get my hands on a gun?", Shaun obnoxiously asks. "Centuries away kid", Sull laughs it off.

Over the upcoming months, more detectives on the Malonie family payroll were getting murdered and having 'R' letters carved on their legs. Razor Rully was playing with his prey. With many officers and detectives fearing their lives they ended their relationships and cut their connections with the Malonies. The Malonies were now truly alone. Was Salvatore right to pull out of the five families to go after the Santanas?

98 Biden Lane Penthouse Block. Roman Santana sits in his penthouse which is one of five in the city. His slickened black beard begins to itch as his associate, Donny, enters with some documents. "I have some files here sir. They contain the information on one Salvatore Malonie", Donny informs. Roman reaches over and flicks through the papers. "What is this? His dating profile? I don't give a shit how old he is or what he fucking does during the day. I want his home, I want his friends, I want what he drives, I WANT his weakness", Roman flips and pulls out his gun shooting Donny. He then stands and kicks his dying employee. "If you want something done I guess you have got to do it yourself", he says.

June 21st. Sull and Henry are watching the news which is reporting; "John Hinckley Jr, the man who attempted to end the life of President Reagan last March, has been found 'not guilty', on the grounds that he is 'insane'". "Absolute load of horseshit", Sull says as he stands disgustedly watching the news. "If he is insane and failed to kill, Jesus Christ, you must be a lunatic brother", Henry, poking fun at his brother, mocks. "You know I was actually in Washington that day and heard the gun shots", Sull educates. "Really? You have only mentioned it like twenty times", Henry sarcastically replies.

Sull was in fact in Washington that day on a job with Serbeano. They had been checked into the Washington Hilton Hotel, where President Reagan was speaking at before his assignation attempt. Sull was driving him and the Don downtown to visit a baker, Kurt Torrez, who had been an old friend of Serbeano's, but had recently been ratted out for calling Serbeano's name to other clients, painting him in an unfair picture.

Sull would take charge of the 'handling' of the Torrez as the Don was unwell in his age and found himself coughing more than speaking. They had pulled up outside the bakery and Serbeano ordered Sull not to kill the man, just to beat him scared. Sull kept his revolver close by anywhere.

The luxurious smell of freshly baked loafs, and warm heat from the oven created a homely atmosphere in the building. A woman and her small child were just getting served by Torrez so Sull pretends to browse for consumer goods until the woman leaves, he didn't want any witnesses. The woman finally leaves with her products and Sull makes his way to the counter to the oblivious Torrez. "How can I help you sir…shit", Torrez says as he lifts his head and realises his boring plain white boxers are about to turn to a dark and disgusting brown stain. Sull grips him tight by the throat and drags him into the back office where he locks himself and Torrez an office room.

As this was happening, around fifty steps away, President Ronald Reagan was just leaving the Hilton Hotel with his entourage, making his way to his vehicle.

Sull bashes Torrez's head against his solid oak desk and throws him viscously back into his seat. He goes into his inner blazer pocket and pulls out a pair of golden brass knuckles. "You are going to pay sweetheart", Sull winks at Kurt. BANG! Six shots go off. Sull, thinking Serbeano may be in danger, runs out of the building. To much of his delight, he is greeted by the sight of the Don stood outside the car holding his revolver. He was about to run in to check if Sull was in danger.

They soon realise, by seeing a flood of swarming citizens running from the sight, that something bigger than them had just nearly happened. They enter the sight of people panicking, people shouting, and agents blocking off the area. They see the president being held by one of his agents, and for a second, Reagan locks eyes with Serbeano. This is a moment Serbeano never forgot.

Salvatore walks through this room, as Sull finishes his story Henry has heard too many times, in order to get into the kitchen. Here he finds Moxie and Michael sleeping on the floor after a heavy night of drinking an unhealthy amount. He immediately calls them into his office disgusted at their actions.

"What are you both thinking? We are in the midst of a war with the Santanas as well as coping with Rully! I need you in the house at all times. Fucking quarantine!", Salvatore raises his voice. Michael takes one look up at his brother and just walks out of the room. "Mox, you can't keep doing this with him. You both are better", Salvatore stands and continues his speech, "we are the future of this family, all three of us. In five to ten years time, we will be the main trio just like our fathers and uncle Arty. It's time you got a grip of that now. Stop the drinking, stop thinking the world is against you both. You have nothing to prove", Salvatore pats his cousin on the back before sending him out.

Across the city, the Santana's had planned their next attack. Thanks to communication with Johnny, who hadn't left New York, the head of the family, Roman, had found out the location of the Malonie home. He plans to send two hitmen tonight on the orders to "take out whoever" they could.

The odds are truly stacked against our Irish-American family. Roman Santana is just as determined and fixed on ending the war than Salvatore was. A true collision of titans is on the horizon. Not only that, but Rully had targeted the law, wiping out the officers on the family payroll. The Malonies are truly standing alone in the heart of a vengeful, blood thirsty hurricane.

There is one last detective still alive on the Malonie payroll, he is the last name on the list. Even though he knows he is probably next after knowing his friends have all been killed. He is the only detective on the list to still keep communications with the family. This detective is Josh Sutcliffe. Josh refused to stay in his office as he knows that something would be in there to kill him, from a possible planted bomb, to his glass of whisky he keeps in his desk draw for the end of the day. Even though he avoided the office he couldn't avoid his fate, he was found dead in his shower later that day.

Meanwhile back in the mansion, Randol made the decision to lift the quarantine that Salvatore had put them under. He felt that by letting the family out it showed face and gave the message to their enemies that they are not scared and won't give in. It was a very old school mentality, the same mentality that Sal felt was killing their family business. This caused a slightly heated argument between Randol and Salvatore. However, Randol was acting as an interim Don until Sal was ready, so he had final say. Michael and Moxie went straight to the clubs.

That night everything would change once again. The old Salvatore that laughed and saw the good in people was set to die. But what was to blame? The old school mentality of the family.

'City's Edge' is the location for Michael and Moxie, they were chatting up a group of single ladies using their name to sell themselves. Five drinks and two lines of 'Charlie's snow' later, the two found themselves in a heart-to-heart conversation. "I get you man, they just look down on me and you, use us for the jobs they can't be arsed to do", Moxie rants. "The reason Ralph is dead is because of their bad planning. I'm always bottom of the line. I should be Don. I've killed more than that golden bollocks prick! I've seen more than him, I belong to this life, he doesn't", Michael shows distain and jealously towards his brother.

To Michael's disgrace, a passing man accidently knocks into him making him spill his drink. Michael spins round and drags the man into the toilets. Moxie follows. Michael smacks the man's head against the sink, cracking his nose. He then yanks the man's head back and smacks it down on the cold tiled ground. Moxie makes sure the cubicles are empty so there are no witnesses. Michael then grabs a bar of soap and rubs it into the man's eyes before stomping on his head eight times. He then picks him up and sits him on one of the toilets in the cubicles before leaving.

Mid-night. Two of the extended family members were patrolling the twenty-acre garden of the mansion but were soon silenced by the Santana hitmen. They infiltrated the **premises** and made their way into the mansion. The bottom floor of the mansion is empty, Michael and Moxie were out, Alexa and Shaun had gone out for a meal, Randol and Lindsey were as sleep, Sull and Henry were playing pool in the basement bar, Martha was reading in bed, Salvatore was in Serbeano's office working, and Lucy was talking to her sister on the bedroom phone.

The hitmen sneak their way upstairs looking to kill the first person they see. They see a bedroom door slightly open. They use their gun to softly creak open the door where they see Lucy in bed on the dial up phone. This was their victim, they both open fire with their silencers equipped. The savages have killed her and her unborn baby. They then make their way back down the stairs where Sull randomly walks ten feet away, they go for Sull but he enters the garage. The hitmen leave.

Cracks in the family further rape the Malonie dynasty.

The days after, Salvatore didn't speak to anyone. His wife, his child, his family in the making had been terrifically stolen from him. He refused to give a speech at the funeral. All his eyes saw was war. The family were all commencing in the 'wake' in the living room when Salvatore walked in with his hair now slicked back in a new style, he wore a new navy-blue suit with a red tie and made a mission statement; "By the end of the year Roman Santana will be dead. Tomorrow we take out his three shops, we burn them to the ground. We then get word to him that we will be at the pub we bought for a 'family occasion'. We will wait for him and fight this war there and then. Then I will personally see to it that Johnny Malonie dies. After that and only after that, we deal with Rully. If you oppose, I don't care leave now. If you're with me, we move tomorrow at 4pm. Henry, I made a call, your son Joey is being released from the army tomorrow and he's in", Salvatore orders and informs. It doesn't take an idiot to realise Salvatore's attitude adjustment, it was clear this was a different man now. "Do we not get to discuss it?", an annoyed Michael asks as he hates the fact his brother is calling the shots. "Did my wife get to discuss to the hitman why she was the victim? Shut the fuck up Michael", Michael was lost for words, up until now Salvatore never communicated in a negative way to his brother. Salvatore Malonie was a changed man. He had lost his whole world. This can only mean one thing and one thing only: war of a gruesome conclusion.

"Do I get to get involved?", an eager Shaun perks up breaking the awkward silence that ensued after Salvatore's snap. "If you have arms and are male, I expect you to be there", Salvatore explains. The family could easily tell that the entire mood of the house had changed, it was the feeling of looming threat. Nobody felt safe and nobody knew what was going to happen next. The family was truly broken.

Salvatore sits in his father's empty office. He pours himself a whisky and rests it on the desk, he doesn't drink it. He is a broken man with a broken family. His only light in this ruthless world had been diffused. He lost his everything.

Martha enters the cold office. "How are you coping son?", she asks, knowing the answer is glum. "We were going to have a girl. A little baby girl", Salvatore begins to wheep. Martha goes over and puts her arms round her baby boy. "We were going to call her Freya, after the Norse Godess of love. She was meant to save me ma", Salvatore breaks down. "How did pops cope with all this death?", he asks wanting an answer to battling grief. "You know something, he never did. You can't. All you can do is keep going. He once told me that grief was like the ocean; it comes on waves ebbing and flowing, sometimes the water is calm, and sometimes it's overwhelming in waves coming in a storm, all we can do is learn to surf them", Martha softly speaks giving Salvatore great comfort.

Michael and Moxie were the ones sent to set ablaze the retail stores owned by the Santana's, there were three in the city. They were on their last one, each hurdled three Molotov's through the shop windows having no regards if people were inside. Michael smiles at the sight of the carnage, he spits on the fire.

From the corner, they are seen by two police officers on patrol. They shout over and chase the two. Michael and Moxie lead them on an intense trail, they lead them through backstreets and alleys. Moxie trips and one officer handcuffs him down. "I'll come back for you when I get your friend you scumbag", the officer says as he leaves Moxie on the floor and continues the chase for Michael. "Lick my ass you dirty pig", Moxie spits back at the officer.

Michael leads them onto a construction site, he reaches the top floor with nowhere to go. On his way up he pushes a dark skinned worker out of the way, this worker follows him up to the top, soon to be, floor. With nowhere to go, Michael has trapped himself on the roof of the early stages of an estate house. The officers reach him and draw their weapons. "Stay right where you are sir!", they shout. "Pigs", Michael responds. The construction worker Michael pushed sneaks behind the officers and takes them out with a metal bar.

"I drive a van, do you need somewhere to go?", the worker asks. Michael looks confused but slightly grateful, he doesn't understand why the gentleman has saved him. Michael takes the weapons from the unconscious officers. "Why did you help me?", he asks. "I recognised you, you're a Malonie. A few years ago, my father was getting abused by pigs in uniform likes these men. The crime he committed, the colour of his skin. Your father, Serbeano, was driving past. He came over and paid the officers to stop beating my father, it was too late however, my father died. I was sat in the back of the car. I saw everything. It was your father who sent me to college", the man opened up. Michael walks over to the man and puts his hand on his shoulders, "I'll take that van", Michael says as his way of a traditional 'thank you'. The worker reveals his name to be Tom.

Tom drives Michael and they pick up the handcuffed Moxie. Michael has Tom drop them off a mile before the mansion to avoid giving away the location. When leaving Michael hands Tom a card with their number on it, "you ever get into any trouble no matter how big or small you give us a call. The Don is now in your debt", he says. Tom hands Michael a card with his number on in return. "I will forever be grateful to your family. If you ever need an extra pair of hands, give me a call", he says.

An hour later, Salvatore led his army of; Michael, Moxie, Sull, Henry, Joey, Shaun, Randol, and a few extras of the extended family friends to their recently bought pub. They all get into positions in the bar, hiding behind and under tables, Sull is placed in the toilets under the orders to open the door when gunfire hits. This was an ambush with destructive intentions. Salvatore was the only man in plain sight, he pours himself a straight vodka and sits on the table, his eyes fixed on the door.

The clock ticks 4.01pm. The door opens and in walks the bulked up, brash, well-dressed, and slickened black bearded Roman Santana in his black overcoat. He appears alone. He sees Salvatore and sits opposite him. Salvatore has given the family orders to open fire on his word. "Well we finally meet", Roman says as he is chewing a golden toothpick. Salvatore takes a swig of his vodka. "Do you not offer me a drink?", Roman rudely asks. Salvatore slides over his vodka in response. Roman finishes it before burping in his face.

"They tell me you're the man to finish the war. I find that insulting but I think to give you a chance, and here I am. I don't see a Don, I don't see a hero. I see a broken failed experiment. You are a disgrace to men like me and today, well today, I put you down sunshine", Roman smiles at Salvatore. Salvatore stays silent and keeps his eyes locked on Roman's. Roman checks his watch. "What is this?", he asks getting fed up with Sal's silent strategy. "The difference between me and you Roman, is that I think when you speak", Salvatore rushes to his feet sending his chair flying back and calls for open fire. The family jump up and start firing, massacring the pub. Roman falls slightly wounded, he calls for his back up. The Santana family rush in from waiting outside and a battlefield takes over happy hour. Salvatore keeps his eyes on Roman and walks through the gun infested battle and makes his way towards the fallen Roman. He kneels in front of him and forces his mouth open, he inserts a small capsule of acid and makes Roman swallow.

The Santana's see this and back off, the Malonies kill two more of their men before they retreat to their cars. Salvatore leads his family to victory as he looks down on Roman who is screaming. Salvatore stands over him and watches him die. And thus, a king is born.

Following this victory, Randol officially made Salvatore Don Malonie. His first act was extremely controversial and something he contemplated for a while now. Salvatore calls Randol, Michael, Moxie and his newly appointed Consigliere, Seth Hemsley, who is a childhood friend of Sal's and is also a professional lawyer, into his new office which was once his father's.

Salvatore first met Seth when he was in kindergarten. Seth's parents, Vino and Karen, were close friends with Serbeano and Martha. They regularly attended double dates with each other. Having worked closely with Vino, Serbeano grew great respect for the man and they soon became close allies. Even though Vino never joined the family business he did often help out on jobs from time to time. The two men always wanted their boys to get along and to much of their delight they did.

They are all stood. Salvatore hands Randol a glass of whisky. "I'm concerned gentlemen, concerned with how we handle business. I have talked with the family, and the family agrees", Salvatore goes over to Randol before continuing, "Randol, you are out. We need to let the past die in order to create the future direction this family wishes to take", a tear comes to Randol's eye as the others feel extreme discomfort between the office walls. Salvatore holds the side of Randol's tearful cheek, "Randy, the first thing you ever taught me is that nobody, nobody is bigger than this family. And this is just business. Randol as of this moment you are relieved of your duties. The family agrees", Salvatore looks down as Randol's eyes are bawling with tears. "We used to be giants, when did we stop?", Salvatore says believing that his family had fallen back and become less powerful than they should be, he blames the old way of doing business of tradition and politics.

Salvatore directs Michael and Moxie out of the room. "You can stay in this house, it is just the business you are no longer part of", Salvatore develops. "It's for the best Randy", he adds. "You have no idea what you have done here today. Who do you think you are? I have served this family all my life, ME AND YOUR FATHER BUILT THIS FAMILY!", a heartbroken Randol shouts. "Randy, it is just business. Times have changed, and the only way we survive is if we do the same", Salvatore enforces. Randol aggressively finishes his drink before leaving the office for the last time.

To a certain extent Randol understood Salvatore's thinking, in order to modernise they have to purge the old school mentality that the family carried. There was a new king in the city now.

That night Salvatore had visited Lucy's grave and took comfort inside the large empty Church, where he sat on the front seats looking up at the large gold cross of Christ. He slowly goes into his pocket and pulls out a small golden engagement ring. Salvatore had planned to propose to Lucy on the night he became Don. That moment had been robbed from him. He looks down at the ring in awe, a tear comes to his eye. "Yes or no? Guess I'll never know", Salvatore softly speaks. "Well Luce, I hope you would have loved the man I have to become", he kisses the ring before putting it back inside his pocket. The Church doors open and in walks an elderly, white haired woman.

The woman sits on the front seats next to where Salvatore is sat. She takes out a packet of tissues and wipes her tearful eyes. The woman looks up and instantly recognises Salvatore from reading about him in the paper a few weeks ago. "Oh my, you are Salvatore Malonie", she exclaims, feeling like she has just seen a celebrity. "Apparently", Salvatore remarks. "Such beautiful eyes, yet they are plagued with sadness. Heavy is the head", she softly speaks.

Salvatore stays silent not wanting to continue the conversation, but the woman is persistent. "Before I lost my husband I never believed in God. But I find that you have to believe in something to keep you going, after all in the darkest hour it is the light at the end of the tunnel that gets you through. But that light is different depending on who you are", she educates. "Tell me Mr Salvatore Malonie, what is your light?", she asks. "I just lost my light", he speaks. "When one light diffuses there will always be another that shines. That gives you energy, that you would give your life for. You just have to look for it", the woman preaches. This sits with Salvatore as it makes him realise that Lucy is gone but his family is still left, and they still need him. Now more than ever. He stands and thanks the woman before leaving.

A few days had passed and the family were starting to get used to Salvatore as the Don. Salvatore was holding a family meeting in the conference room of the mansion. This is where all the business went down. Sull, Henry, Joey, Michael, Moxie, and Seth were in attendance. Salvatore explained to his empire that he wanted Johnny Malonie dead, but he was seeing to that personally. He also has plans to advance on Razor Rully. He knew that this wasn't easy and it was more of a case of waiting for Rully to find them as Razor went off the grid. "We can't just sit like ducks waiting for bread, we need to go out looking", Michael, to no one's surprise, disagreed with his brother. Moxie supported Michael. "We wait. He will come to us", Salvatore defends his decision. Michael smacks down on the table and leaves. "Where are you going?", a furious Salvatore asks knowing that rebellion will make him look as a weak leader. "Off to find Rully", Michael remarks before Moxie gets up and follows him. "Sull, tail them", Salvatore orders to make sure no harm, or more importantly, no harm gets committed by the two rebels.

Salvatore kept his operation of dealing with Johnny Malonie to himself and himself only because he wanted to deal with a family traitor on his own grounds. It was too personal, and he wanted to use Johnny as an example to anyone out there wanting to initiate a war with his family. If he could do damage to his own blood it would make randomers second guest coming for them. His other order of business was getting back in the five families, he only left to avoid a war within the group as they refused permission to kill Santana. Despite what Randol believes, he fully understood the importance of the families.

It didn't take long for Michael and Moxie to arrive at the Rully's private club, 'City's Edge'. However, they were unsurprisingly refused entry. Michael headbutted the bouncer and the two made their way in. Problem solved.

Shoving every dancer out of their way, they made their way to the bar where they came across a blonde bar maid named Kenna. "Hey darling I'm here to see your scumbag boss", Michael declared. "Not possible sugar-tits", Kenna, realising the aggressive nature of Michael, responds verbally slaying the mafia man. "What did you just say!?! Does she know who she is talking to?", Michael asks Moxie. "Show her Mikey", Moxie encourages Michael who leans over and grabs Kenna's ponytail and presses her head against the bar, prompting the attention of a seven-foot bouncer on the dancefloor.

The bouncer storms over and grabs Michael by the back of the neck dragging him off the bar maid. Kenna then throws a glass of ice-cold water over the gangster. Moxie goes to kick the bouncer but falls and crashes onto the floor.

Thankfully, Sull has made his way in and pays the bouncer off. He grabs Michael and verbally attacks them both. "You think this is something Serb and Randy would have done? You are reckless, this is why he ordered a hit on Rully those years ago. Keep going the way you are, and you'll end up just like him, is that what you want?", Sull slaps them both as they don't answer. "Is that what you want?", he repeats. Moxie shakes his head. "Mike, what about you?", Sull asks a second time preparing to drop him if he fails to answer again. "No", Michael reluctantly wrestles out of his mouth.

As Sull releases Michael, over in the outskirts of the city in the Malonie mansion, a letter has arrived for Salvatore. He opens it alone in his office. He is suspicious as he wasn't accepting anything. It is a handwritten letter, instead of ink it was pig's blood. He knew straight away this was from Rully. 'Dear Sal, Mr Malonie it has been a while, I'm guessing you know I'm in the city. Heck I am the city. I want you to know that killing you brings me such pain so just know its business nothing personal kid. Between now and next Tuesday, you will be dead. Then I have fulfilled the vendetta. I wanted to send my condolences to you, I'm sorry to hear about your girl but I read in the paper you won the 'blood grudge', so I guess it's fair. See you around baby-cakes, love R. Rully'. Salvatore burns the letter.

At this point Seth enters the office with some news that is likely to delight Salvatore. "Boss, we have a possible location on Johnny. Rico saw him downtown at the old gym, looks like he's been living there", Seth informs. "And that's where he dies", Salvatore loads up his revolver. "What should I do about the rest?", Seth, wanting to know what he tells the family, wonders. "Tell them I'm taking care of business", Salvatore says as he is about to leave. He then stops and turns back to Seth, "arrange a phone call with the five families, tell them I want to talk business and that Rully is dead", Seth looks confused. "But he's still alive Sal", he is baffled. "But the time I see the families he will be dead", Salvatore leaves the room and embarks on his mission to deal with Johnny Malonie.

Martha greets him at the door having just overheard the conversation. She doesn't want him to kill Johnny as killing blood is something Serbeano would have never even contemplated. "Sal, don't do what I think you are going to do", Martha puts her hand on her son to stop him. Salvatore grabs her hand softly, "Mother, this man put all of us at risk, if I don't do this now it might happen to us", Salvatore spoke. "We don't kill blood", Martha simply replied. "Well, I do", Salvatore, fixed with determination on his mission, says. "Send him away, beat him, but do not kill him". Salvatore was getting annoyed at his mother's persistency. "He sided with the man that killed Uncle Art, how can you possibly defend him. Innocent people die every day, but heartless fiends like him live. It's not right, I'm bringing balance", Salvatore's final words before softly brushing past his mother to leave.

The old rundown gym was in the heart of Brooklyn Heights, one of the roughest areas in the city. Salvatore pulled up around the back of the building not to alert Johnny. He then snook around the front and was met face to face with the front door.

Salvatore knew that going through this door, he wouldn't be able to return. The minute he steps through he has to kill his own blood. He had reached a point of no return. He takes one deepening breath, withdraws his revolver and enters.

Mould and dampness populate the atmosphere, he walks up some creaky wooden stairs that lead to the main gym area. Old bench press benches, rotting pull down machines, and old but fierce weights sit collecting dust having last served their purpose in 1980. Salvatore sees an old office across the room, 'this must be where Johnny is', thinks Salvatore.

He quietly opened the door to find a sleeping Johnny on the desk. He holds up his gun to his head but finds himself not being able to pull the trigger. He wants Johnny alive to feel the pain his family felt by the betrayal.

Johnny wakes and falls off the desk at the sight of the raging Salvatore. "Sal, Sal, what are you doing?", Johnny pleads for his life. "I have come to kill you Johnny", Salvatore deviously declares. "Sal please, no you don't understand!", Johnny's knees are shaking. "You betrayed the family Johnny. They gave you a chance to leave and you didn't. You're done Johnny", Salvatore is ready to kill. "Please Sal I'll do anything, I can tell you where Razor is", this stops Sal. "He plans to kill you at midnight tonight, he was going to storm your weapons factory and wait for you there", Johnny who is now physically begging cries. "Get up. GET UP!", shouts Salvatore. Johnny uses the desk to pick himself up. "You're coming with me. If he doesn't show I will kill, if he does, well let's just hope I don't get trigger happy", Salvatore grabs Johnny and drags him into his car as they make their way to the mansion.

Salvatore locks Johnny in the car, since he got shot in the leg by Randol, he is unable to move far anyway. Salvatore calls for a family meeting where he explains the next plan. He plans the hit on Razor Rully that his father failed. He will wait in the factory. The family will hide in the factory and ambush just like in the pub. "We have men but not enough, the Rully's are the most viscous type of people out there. If anyone knows anybody who would be willing to take a bullet for us get them", Salvatore stands at the head of the table as he explains. "What about the families", Henry enquires. "No. We do this without them, we are proving a point", Salvatore replies much to the distain of his brother. "We meet here with our men at 10pm tonight", his final orders.

Once the meeting concluded, Michael called Tom and got him recruited. "Say your goodbyes, this is a war I don't expect this room to be filled with the same amount of people in twelve hours time", Salvatore's words lingered in heads of each member of the family. Salvatore approaches Alexa and Shaun, he informs them both they are now officially part of the family business as he hires Alexa as his secretary, and Shaun as a soldier. They are both delighted especially

Shaun who has a grin a mile long. Moxie embraces his father for what could be the last time, Sull and Henry share what could be one last beer in the basement. Martha embraces her boys for what could be the last time.

Salvatore feels he needs to do one more thing, if he doesn't, he might regret it. He calls Michael into his office.

Salvatore offers Michael to sit but he chooses to stand. "There wasn't a day that went by where I didn't think about you when I was over in London", he goes into his blazer and pulls out a pile of letters. "I wrote you fifty letters, each one got sent back to me. They didn't want anything Razor could trace me on", he slides over the letters to Michael. "You're my brother. I think the world of you", Salvatore says.
Michael is speechless as he opens the letters. Salvatore could see the regret and sadness in his eyes. "I want you to know that if we survive tonight, I have great plans for you brother. But you got to meet me halfway, stop the drink, stop the negativity. Be my brother again", Salvatore stands and leaves to let it all sink into Michael's stubborn brain. A tear comes to Michael's eyes.

10pm. the Malonies find themselves in an army of twenty-five, Salvatore goes around and shakes the hand of each one. Tom is among them. He has one final speech to lead his family to victory. "We lost.

Each and every one of us in this room tonight has lost in some way because of Razor Rully. No longer we fear that name, no longer we wait. Tonight is for all those we lost, tonight is for the future of this family. We will not lay down to fear! Make every bullet count", Salvatore declares.

The Malonie troopers are in position, Salvatore stood in plain sight in the middle of the factory. He has Johnny on his knees in front of him with his revolver pointed at his head. The clock strikes midnight, they hear the sound of two cars pull up outside. Many feet scatter the outside ground. The next few minutes are the most intense any man had ever felt, the suspense was earth shattering.

Their surroundings began to shake and vibrate. Salvatore suspected something was wrong but before he could act they are all sent hurdling to the floor. Rully's men had sent two bulldozers into the building from left to right. They had already taken over the factory this morning. Johnny had led Salvatore into a trap. Rully had taken the factory this morning…

It was 10am, Hunter had strolled through the factory doors and shot a gun up in the air to halt the workers. "This establishment is under new management", the workers stood confused at Hunter. The doors sprung wide open and in strolls the cowboy boot wearing Razor Rully. He wears a cowboy hat, chews a toothpick, and spits out of his dark blonde bearded mouth. He is dressed as a cowboy. His eyes are those that belong to great white sharks, doll like and only see destruction. Nothing else. "Rejoice blue collar workers, we come with great news", he echoes. Hunter slaps down his briefcase and pulls out fake documents that show that Rully now 'owns' the factory. "Now not all of you will survive this transition so we are going to ask you all to line single file in front of my briefcase to reveal if you made the cut so to speak", Hunter informs. The workers reluctantly line up. Hunter flips up the top of the briefcase and holds up, not to the knowledge of the work force, a tommy gun. He blasts them all dead, sending bullets flying straight through them all like a game of dominos. Razor laughs at the sight. It is important to note that Johnny was also in attendance, he knew Salvatore was leading his family into a trap.

The family get up in the ambush. Rully's men raid the factory and an all-out gun war has broken lose. Bullets flying everywhere. Salvatore picks himself up and searches around. He came to kill Rully, and either him or Rully wouldn't walk out here alive.

Bodies starting to populate the floor, Salvatore walks over them in pursuit to find Rully. Meanwhile back in the top balcony of the factory, Michael and Tom are fighting side by side taking out Rully's men left right and centre, Sull, across from them, is wrestling one of the men. The man kicks him through the barrier and he falls down ten foot landing hard on one of the workstations. Henry runs over and tackles the man before strangling him taking his life.

Salvatore sees the **silhouette** of Rully in the distance, he grips his gun tight and makes his way over. BOOM! The factory becomes engulfed in unforgiving flames as one of the bulldozers caught ablaze. "GET OUT! GET OUT!", Salvatore orders his men to retreat. Standing opposite him in the blaze stands Razor Rully who has a vengeful smile and look in his eyes. This was the stand-off five years in the making, the true battle for king, vengeance, and survival. Last man standing.

"How I've waited for this", Rully says. "I'm flattered", Salvatore remarks sarcastically. The two raise their guns, Salvatore fires first but has run out of bullets. He runs over, Rully sees this and throws down his loaded gun wanting to fight Malonie fist on fist. Salvatore dives on Rully grounding them both. They fight launching fists onto each other, they brawl all over as the fire rises.

"You're just like your father, all spirit no heart", Razor spits in Salvatore's face. Rully begins to choke Sal. "You won't win", Salvatore is barely able to breathe let alone speak. "Look around you, we aren't getting out of here alive sunshine", Rully laughs. Salvatore begins to fade. He sees flashes in his head. He is stood at the alter with Lucy, he is hugging his mother when he returned home. Then he sees his father, who stands before him and grabs his head, "you have done me proud son, finish this war", a tear falls from Sal's eye, he has failed his father. Rully had him killed.

Out of nowhere Michael throws himself at Rully forcing him to release Salvatore and save him the second he was about to die. Salvatore coughs up and picks himself up as he sees Rully brawling with his brother. He sees Rully's dropped revolver in the distance, does he help his brother or go for the gun?

He rushes over for the gun hoping that Michael keeps in the fight. He quickly picks up the 'R. Rully' engraved revolver and shoots Rully in his spineless back. Rully shouts out in pain before falling off Michael, he is still alive and blood pours through his mouth. Rully begins to crawl around gasping and gripping onto his life with all his energy in his body. Salvatore picks his brother up and the two stand over Rully. "Let go Rully, you're not welcome here", Salvatore's chilling last words as Rully turns his head looking him directly in the eyes. Salvatore fires the gun and kills the savaged fiend.

The two brothers make their way out of the fiery abyss where they are reunited with their family. The Malonie's lost two men in the battle, two men of the extended family, and Sull was heavily injured knowing that he will never be able to walk again properly on his left leg as a result of his tertius tumble.

A deep thought kept racing through Salvatore's mind though. Although he had just killed Razor Rully he knew he had some lose ends to cut. For example, Santino Rully was still active. It was also later revealed that Johnny Malonie's body was not discovered in the debris after police and forensics surveyed the area. This was a problem.

"We have checked through the carnage and accumulated an amount of 17 bodies discovered. This gang warfare must and will end, I have made it my personal mission to bring New York to the gang free powerhouse it used to be", says the voice of the freshly appointed head of police, detective Brody Harper on the news. Brody was called in to 'fix' the gang situation in the city, he is under the orders to stay in New York until he does. He was coming for the Malonies and the rest of the five families. He wants to reshape the city and will stop at nothing until he does.

Back in the Malonie mansion, Salvatore has called Tom into his office where he is given a glass of whisky and ordered to sit. "Tom, I want to thank you for your service in the fight today. I would like to personally welcome you into the family", Salvatore shakes Tom's hand having great respect for him. "Thank you Salvatore", Tom is elated. "I understand you have a son and wife. We will take care of them. I also have a point of business to appoint you", Tom is eager to know what. "I want you to lead my business in narcotics. This family has always avoided touching this business. However, now is the time. We can make huge profit on this stuff. My only demand is that the family don't touch it, that includes you. Nobody takes this, we just sell. The minute drugs get involved it gets messy. All we do is transport them one place to another and sell. Seth will give you all the details later, don't let me down Tom", Salvatore gives Tom a great opportunity which he accepts with great gratitude.

Serbeano was given the opportunity to set up a narcotics business expansion but he always refused. He believed, like Salvatore, that the minute you get drugs involved the business gets messy and defeats itself eventually.

54 miles east, the fugitive Johnny Malonie has boarded a plane in an attempt to flee the city and leave his past behind. He boards the empty plane and figures its weird, but he sits down and reads the magazine. He becomes increasingly more suspicious as nobody else has boarded the plane and it's now on the runway. He gets ready to stand up when the plane hits the runway and breaches into the atmosphere. He panics and runs over to a flight attendant who sits him back down. The pilot doors fly open and out walks Hunter and Santino Rull who make their way to

Johnny. Johnny's heart is racing. Will they kill him? Will they crash the plane? How will he get out of it?

"Johnny Malonie, you got somewhere to be?", Santino mocks. "He looks like he is running Sonny", Hunter, encouraging the mocking, states. "I would if I were him. He lost his family, his home, and his wife. When you came to me those months ago, I saw untouched potential. Now I realise I was blinded. All I see is a weak waste of skin", Santino spits his toothpick at Johnny's face. "You don't run from me kid", Santino claims as he leans over to Hunter to check Hunter's watch. "In around five minutes you will be dropped in these waters, straight into the home of at least three great white sharks", he grabs Johnny's head and pulls it close. "You don't fuck with me", he spits in rage. "I helped you, just let me leave", Johnny, finally breaking his silence, pleads. "Your family gave you that option, it clearly didn't work", Santino slams Johnny back in his seat as Hunter drags him off by his ear over to the emergency door.

The wind rapes Johnny's face of regret, he always did hate heights. Hunter grabs tight to the window as he pushes Johnny straight down to the sharks. Was this the last of Johnny Malonie?

Back in the safety of Salvatore's warming office, Sal is informed of the news that 'Johnny Malonie has been taken care of', he figures it was Rully's doing. He celebrates by pouring himself a whisky. The good news is short lived though as Seth informs him that the five families have declined Salvatore's request to re-join as he has broken their trust. "They will need money, offer them $50,000. Take it from my personal account", Salvatore hopes to buy his way back into the union.

Alexa, Shaun, Michael, Moxie, Joey, Tom, Sull, and Henry are gathered in the office as Salvatore had called for a meeting. He is sat at his desk with a black case in front of him. He calls for Seth to open it up. There are nine silver rings. Each ring has a small red sword in the middle, this sword is representative of the Irish God, Lugh.

They all place their rings on. "When people see this ring, I want them to see power, and an unbreakable bond", Salvatore declares as he places his on.

In the months that came up, Santino Rully had moved to California LA. The five families accepted Salvatore' $50,000 and he was back. The Malonies were back on top. Power had been re-established once more in the Malonie empire.

New Year's Eve 1982. Salvatore, with Seth by his side, attended his first meeting of the five families as the Don. Salvatore was explaining his plan to expand to Nevada Las Vegas to tap into the casino business. The other families were cautious about the move as Vegas were ran by the Ferguson's, and nobody challenged the Ferguson's, they ran the strip. Salvatore hoped to collaborate for this operation and work alongside the Sutcliffe family, as he wanted to give something back to them as their family member was detective Josh Sutcliffe, who Rully murdered.

The family disapprove but Salvatore, if he wants to successfully take Vegas, needs their backing. He will upset a lot of people with this move. He looks them in their eyes intensely, "I sat in this room a few months ago and told you all, to your faces, I was going to kill Roman Santana with or without your support. Exactly twenty-one days after that statement I personally took the life of Roman Santana", he takes a drink then continues; "I then waged war with Razor Rully, the very man my father and you all failed to take down. I am the man who personally put a bullet in his head. They called me crazy, even my family doubted me. When I say something, I deliver and believe me when I say, I am taking Vegas", Salvatore, proudly and firmly speaks.

The families think over Salvatore's words before Mark Sutcliffe speaks up and agrees. "We will go into business, on the condition that if I wish to pull out, I am able to with no consequences. Me and my wife Donna will fly out and live there", Mark and Salvatore shake hands. "Happy new year gentlemen", Salvatore is delighted and excited for the future.

Salvatore arrives back at the mansion to the sight of his family partying in anticipation of 1983. Music is bouncing, foods is being devoured, booze is being drank. Salvatore walks through straight into his office. He sits at his desk and admires his photo of his father sat at the desk. He smiles.

Michael knocks and enters. "You said you wanted to see me when you came back", Michael says before sitting opposite his brother. "Brother, we are taking Vegas. I want you to lead that operation. January 4$^{th}$ you fly out and live there. I am putting my trust in you so don't let me down", Salvatore says to the ecstatic Michael who couldn't be happier. He stands and offers his hand out to his brother. "This is a new beginning Mike, don't waste it", Salvatore says shaking his hand. "Thank you, brother". That was the first time Michael had acknowledged Salvatore as his brother since his return. Salvatore believed that by Moxie being an 'enabler' and a lap dog to Michael, it was weighing him down and making him worse, so he just sends Michael to Vegas and keeps Moxie here in New York. He thinks it will benefit them both by keeping them apart as they are like two naughty school children when they are together.

After Michael leaves the office, Randol soon enters. "I just wanted to say Sal, your father would be proud. I'm sorry I doubted you about the families", Randol apologises. "There's no need to apologise Randy, the whole world doubted me", Salvatore says as Randol steps back and smiles. "You have his spirit. I look forward to see where you take this family, Don Malonie", Randol raises his glass of red wine to his nephew. "Me and you both Randy", Salvatore raises his small glass of whisky. Martha comes in and drags the two out as the countdown begins, "10,9,8" Salvatore looks around at his family, Shaun holding Alexa, Sull and Henry half cut with their arms around each other swaying, Lindsey and Randol holding each other, "7, 6, 5, 4:, Michael stood messing with Moxie's tie to annoy him, and Martha who is stood armed with a cherry. This is his family, he wouldn't change them for the world, he will protect them at all costs. They were his light. Family is everything. "3, 2, 1". HAPPY NEW YEAR! 1983 had arrived.

Salvatore slips away from the celebrations and regathers his thoughts in his office, he closes the door and stands alone. He can't get Lucy out of his head. He misses her ocean eyes he used to get trapped in, he lusted for one more time seeing her comb her hair first thing in the morning, he missed the way her ever expensive perfume smelt when she walked past. But most importantly, he missed his best friend. He wonders what he would be like as a father and how now, he may never get that chance. His soul is broken.

His desk office phone starts to ring. "Salvatore Malonie?", the voice of Mark Sutcliffe speaks. "Live and in colour Mr Sutcliffe", Salvatore responds, clearing his throat breaking him from his trance of stolen love. "I will be bringing twenty men with me to Nevada, are you ready to take Vegas?", Mr Sutcliffe asks. "I'm ready to take Vegas Mr Sutcliffe,"…

**The Malonies will return…**

*Credits to Mark Sutcliffe and Donna Sutcliffe for helping me proofread

*Credits to Chad James for making a poster to help me promote

Thank you for reading.

*"Never assume that loudest person in the room is the strongest, they are often the weakest"*

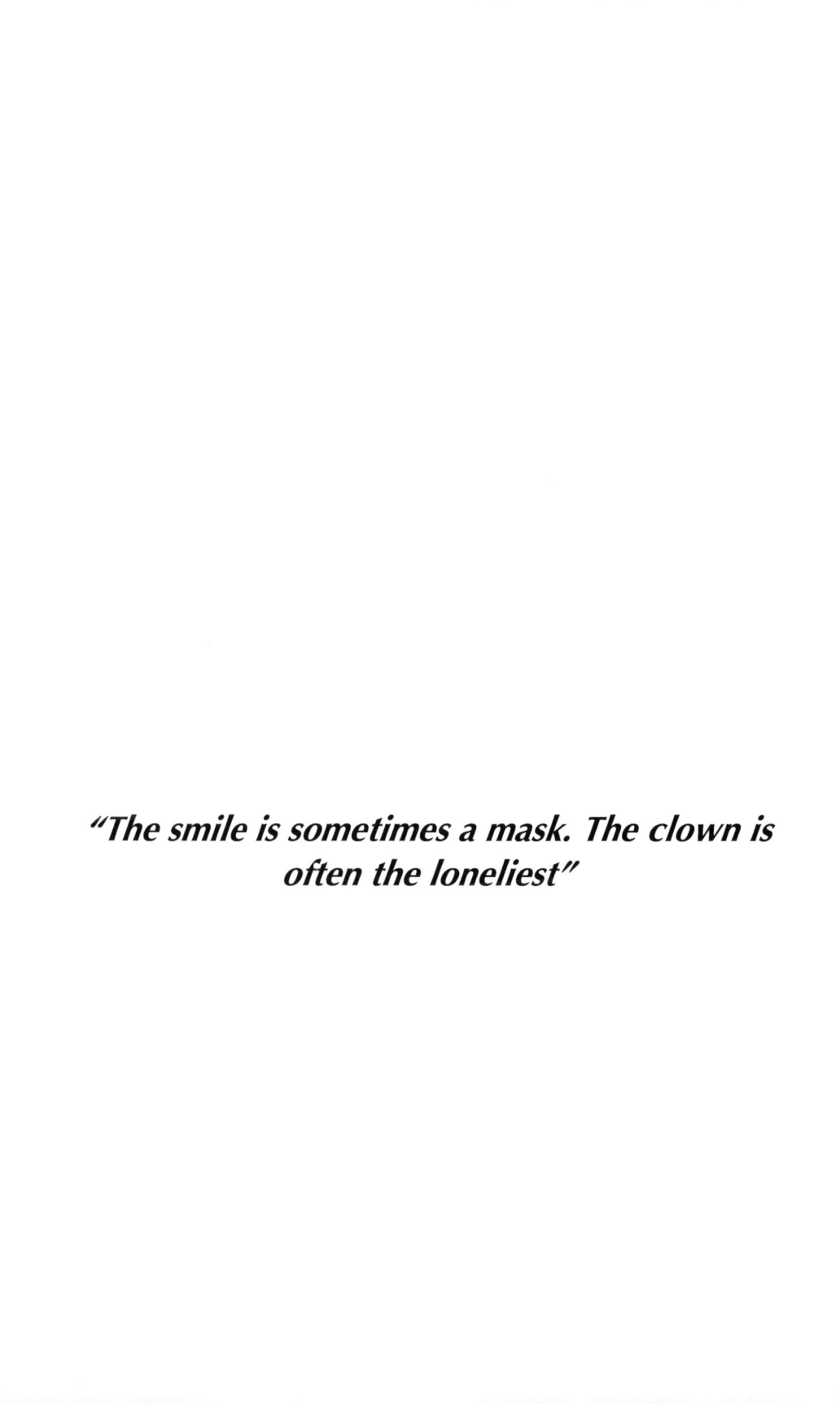

*"The smile is sometimes a mask. The clown is often the loneliest"*

*"Be you and you only"*

*"Make your smile change the world"*

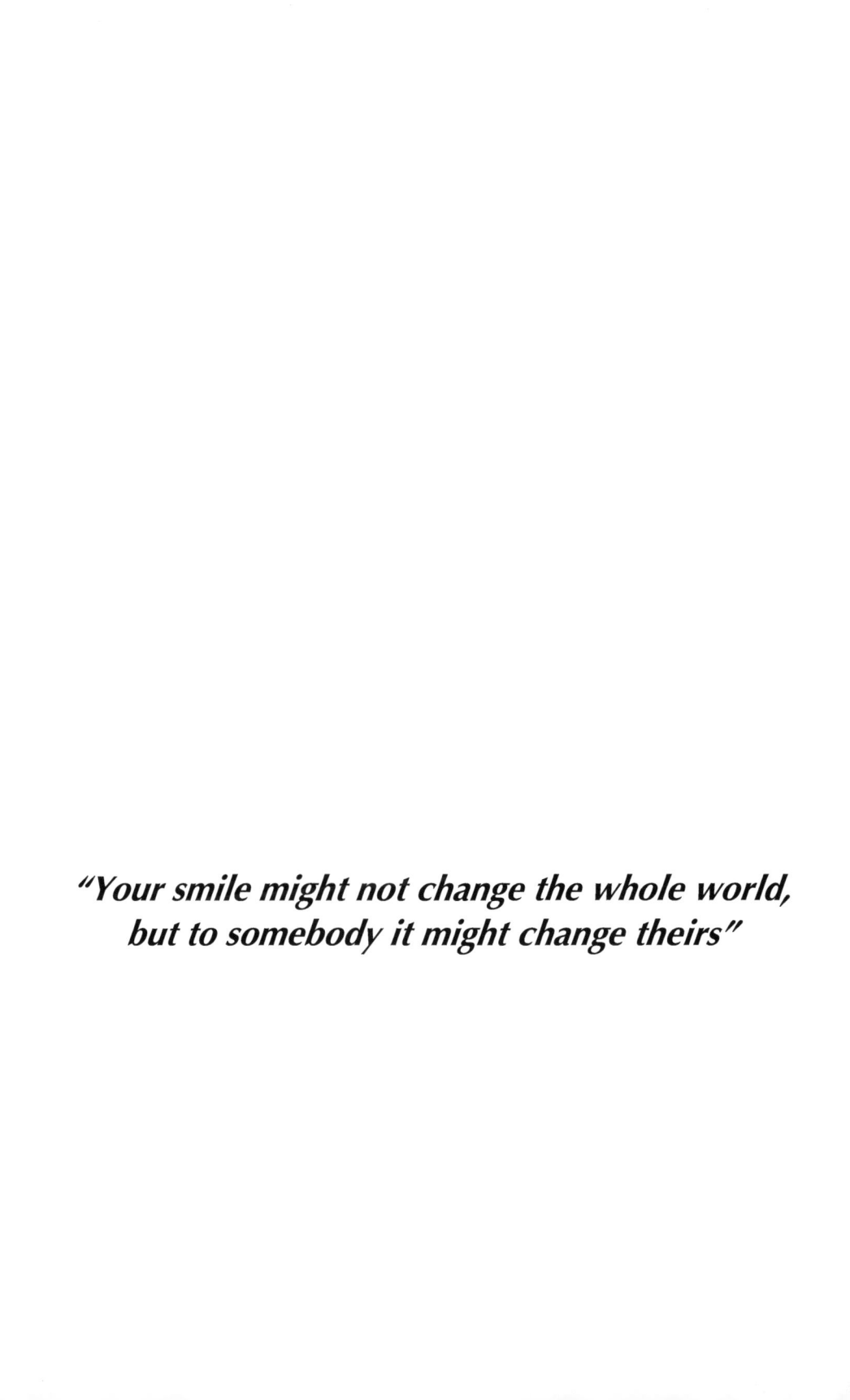

*"Your smile might not change the whole world, but to somebody it might change theirs"*

*"Live. Love. Laugh"*

*"Never lose, just learn"*

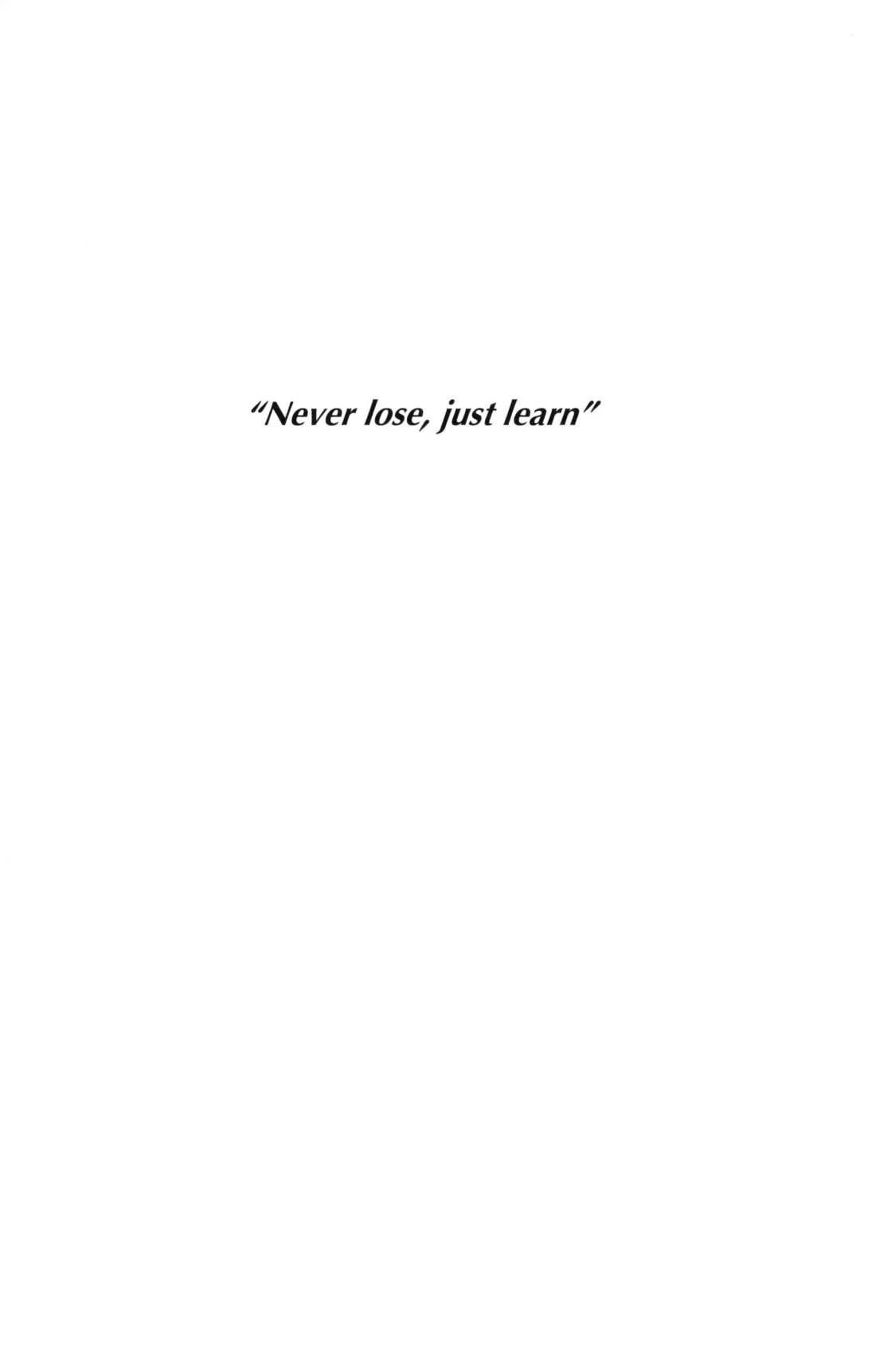

*"Don't put off today what you can do tomorrow"*

*"Never fail"*

*"Be the person your future child will be proud of"*

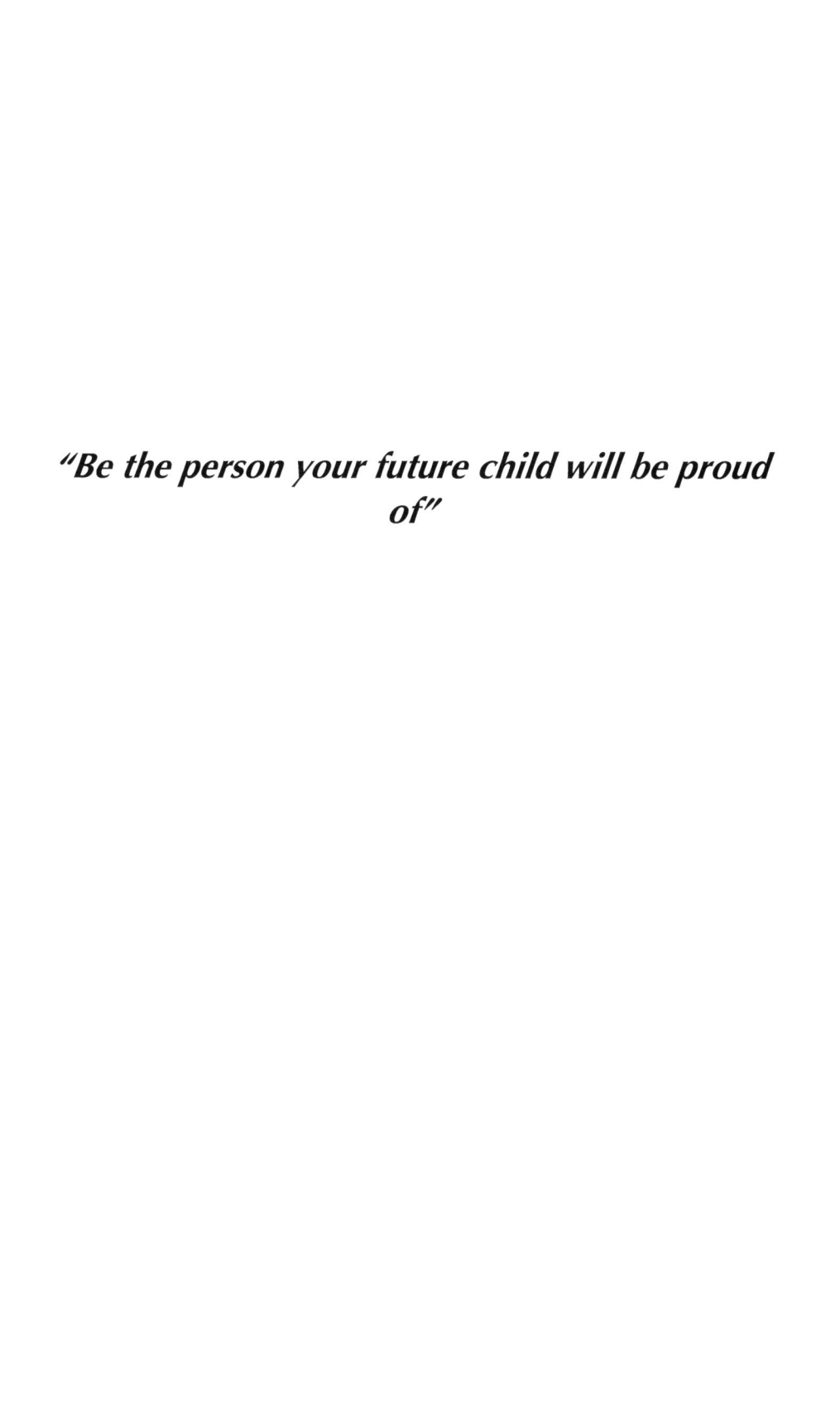

*"Live to laugh"*

*"Dare to dream, risk to win"*

*"Never let anyone abuse your trust. It's a matter of dignity"*

*"Be the one"*

*"Stand for what you believe in and have faith in others"*

*"Togetherness"*

*"Never stop creating your best self"*

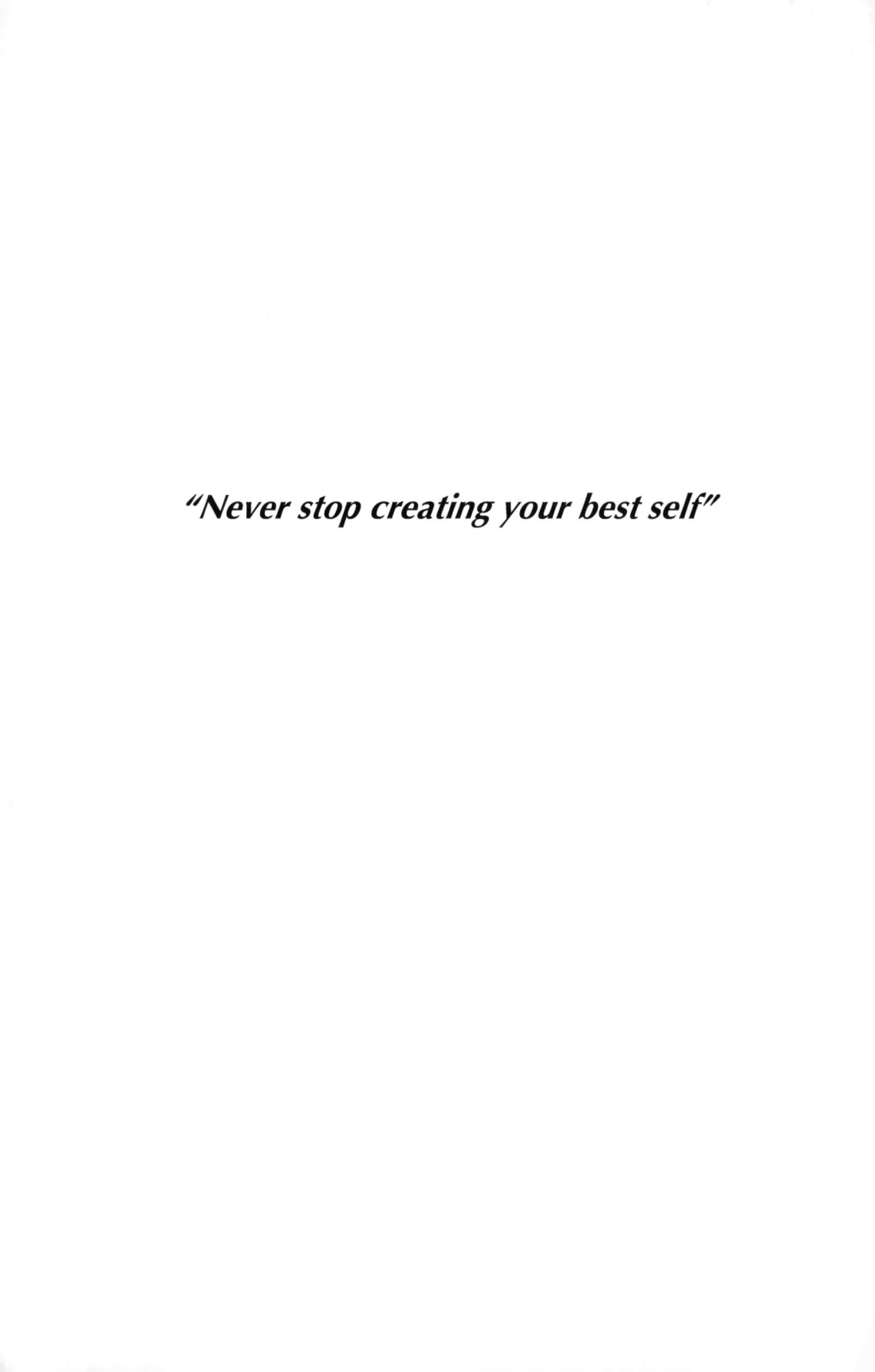

*"Mistakes happen, we are human"*

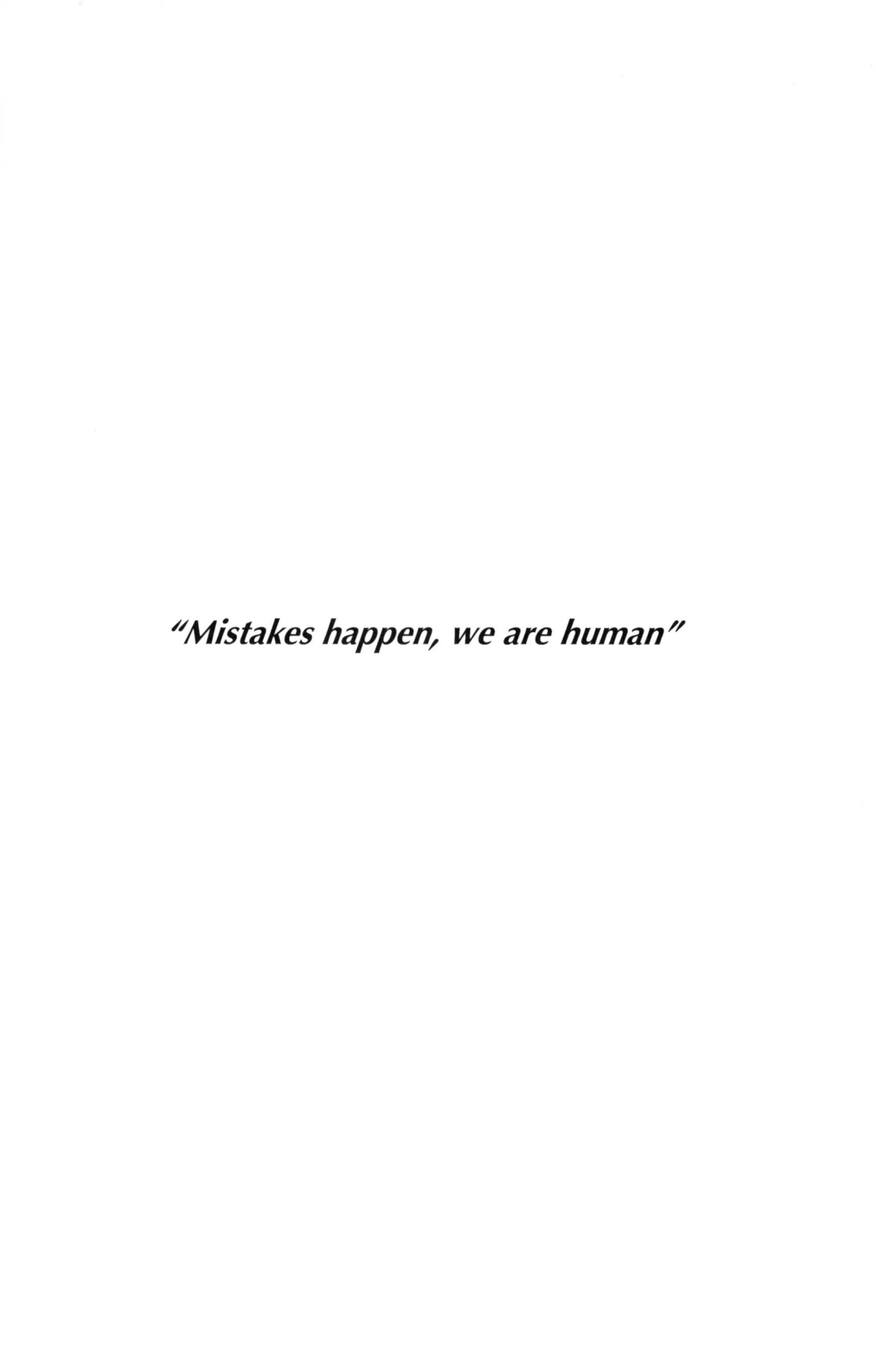

*"The storm comes before the rainbow shines"*

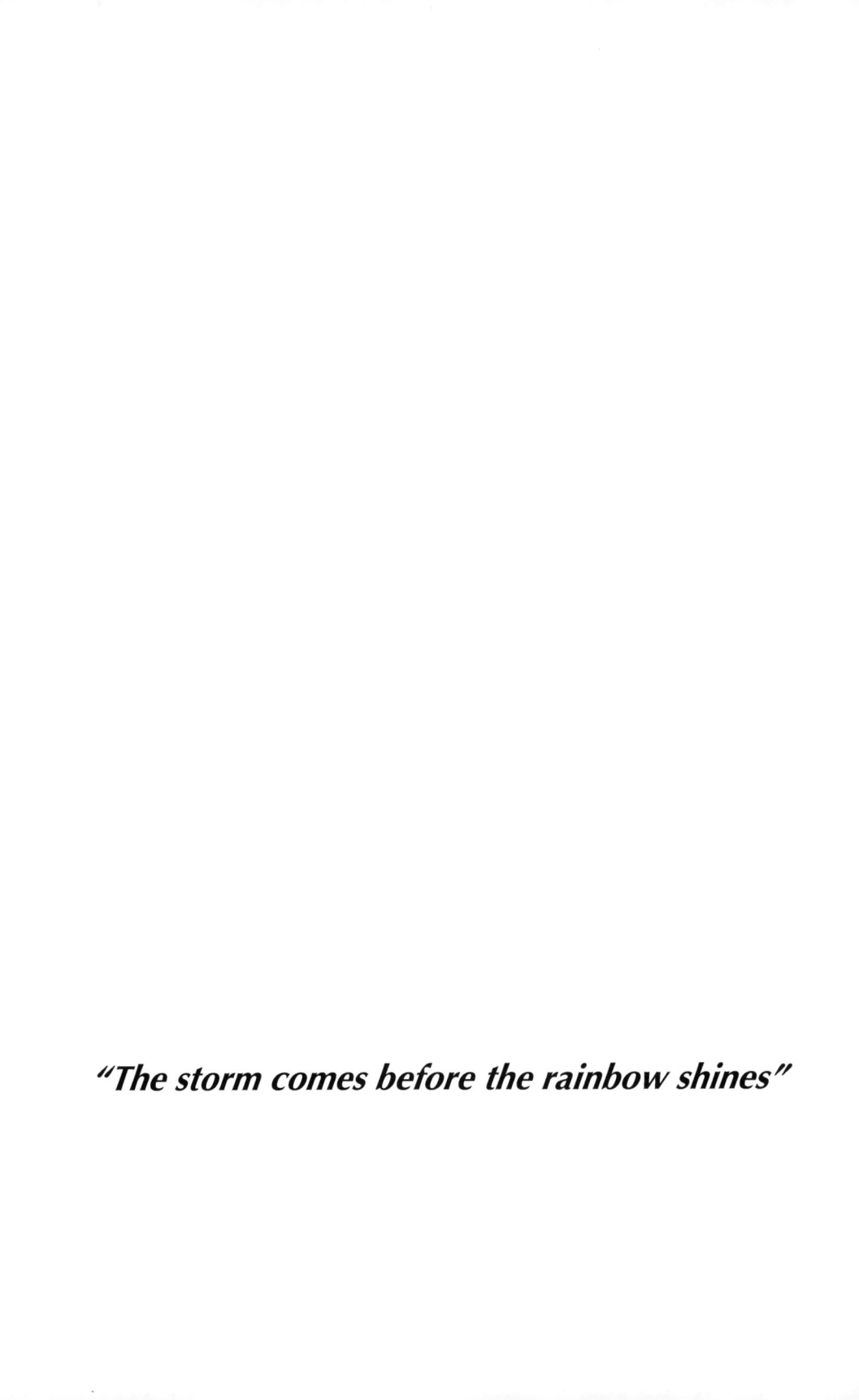

*"To live in the past is to die in the future"*

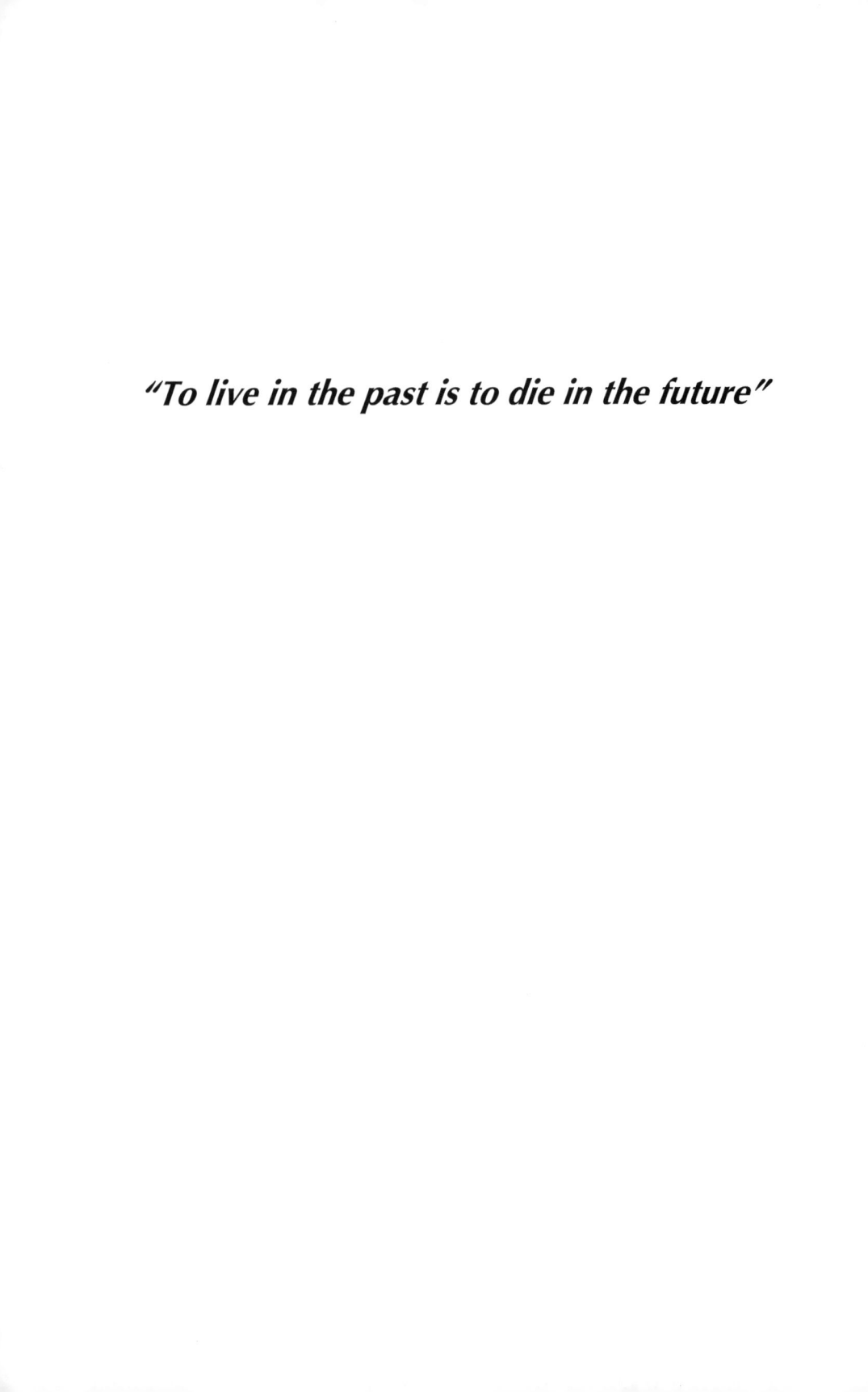

*"Make yourself good enough"*

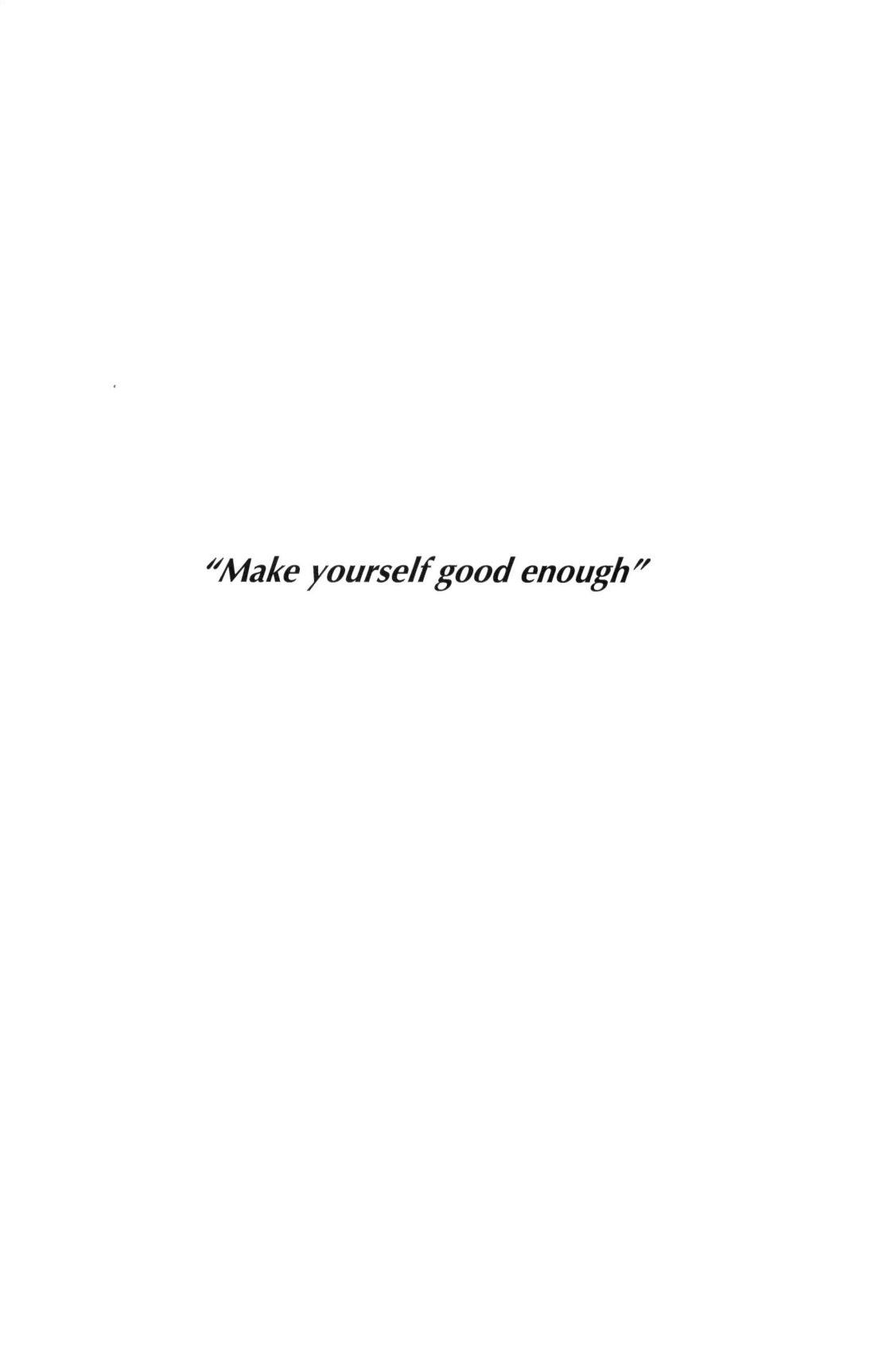

*"Respect and hustle"*

Printed in Great Britain
by Amazon